# THE OUT IS DEATH

Peter Rabe worked for much of his life as a professor of psychology. Donald Westlake has written that "the understatement of violence" in Rabe's novels, "resulting from his modesty of character rather than modesty of experience," culminated in a method that "was refined...to a laconic hipness I could only admire from afar." Rabe published his unique brand of crime novels for twenty years, from 1955 to 1974. He lives in southern California.

# THE OUT IS DEATH

**PETER RABE**

Black Lizard Books
Berkeley • 1988

 For information contact: Black Lizard Books, 833 Bancroft Way, Berkeley, CA 94710. Black Lizard Books are distributed by Creative Arts Book Company.

ISBN 0-88739-093-5
Library of Congress Catalog Card No. 87-72696

Manufactured in the United States of America

## *Chapter 1*

THE TIGHT OVERCOAT gave him the long shape of a tube and he walked bent forward to keep the rain out of his face. He walked fast and it showed his age. Once he stopped to take a deep breath, and then moved on again. He crossed the street without looking up.

There was a place near the corner with gold letters on grimy glass which said *Sport Parlor*. Through the glass a room showed dimly, a room with a jukebox that made silent flashes, and two men at the edge of a pool table. The men smoked and made gestures which seemed meaningless unaccompanied by the sounds of their voices. They both looked out to the street, and one man pursed his mouth to let his cigarette drop to the floor. He stepped on it with a quick twist of his heel and he laughed in pantomime. Then he walked out onto the street.

He zipped up his jacket, hunched his shoulders when the drizzle hit him, and ran to his car. The car glittered with rain and chrome and leaped away from the curb almost as soon as the door flew shut.

The old man stopped at the bus sign and stood near the curb. His hand was on the post of the sign and he looked tired. He was standing like that when the car shot close. The car squealed and stopped spectacularly, splashing the old man from the waist down.

"Hey, Dalton! You get wet?"

The man in the car put his head out of the window. He

looked at the old man and laughed. The sound was unfriendly.

"Hey Dalton—"

The old man had not moved and his hand was still clasped tightly around the post. Then he let go of it and wiped his face.

"What?" he said. "What now?"

The man in the car opened the door and got out in a single quick movement.

"Hey, Dalton," he said again. "You going someplace? You're not going far, are you, Dalton?"

The old man stepped back a little, because the other man had stepped very close. The other man was holding onto the old man's coat and Dalton could not step back very far.

"I'm taking the bus," he said. "I'm just taking the bus downtown." Then he pushed the other man's hand away from his coat.

"You look sick, Dalton," said the other man. "All this running around outdoors after ten years indoors." He laughed. "That ain't healthy." He took the old man's coat again and smiled. "You wouldn't do anything unhealthy, would you, Dalton?"

Dalton pushed the hand away again and watched his bus splash down the street.

"Dicky," he said, "it's noon and you gave me until evening. I said this evening."

"You look awful tricky to me, Dalton. I don't know if I can afford to let you wait till evening."

Dalton watched the bus come nearer. He tried to step to the curb but Dicky got in his way.

The old man wasn't afraid, but he felt weak. He only wanted to avoid friction, and to get his bus.

"I said tonight, Dicky. You ever know me to cross anyone up?"

"You been in stir so long, Dalton, I think maybe you changed. I don't know any more what goes on in your head."

"Lemme go," said Dalton, and tried to wave at the bus.

Dicky held down the old man's arm.

The bus was very close now and both men could see the driver. The driver did not know whether or not the men at the stop were fares.

"Damn it, I can't miss it," Dalton began, but Dicky laughed and shook his head at the bus.

The old man cursed softly, and watched the bus go on past down the street. The fat tires squished through a puddle and then started to sing against the wet asphalt.

Dicky got back into his car and cupped his hands to light a cigarette. He watched the old man over his hands and his eyes crinkled. Then he laughed through a big billow of smoke.

"I trust you, Dalton. I was just kidding around."

Dalton said nothing.

"Remember how you and me used to kid around, Dalton? You don't kid much no more, do you? That last stretch really rocked you, huh?" Dicky gunned the motor a couple of times, but he did not seem to be in a hurry to leave.

"Dalton," he called from the car.

The old man ignored him.

Dicky backed up the car with a sudden bounce and stopped it in front of the old man.

"Kidding time is over, huh, Dalton?" Dicky shifted, held the clutch. "Just don't you forget it," he said. The way the car shot off, it seemed angry.

The old man did not watch the car out of sight. He closed his eyes and ran both hands over his face. The gesture smoothed his face for a moment, making him look the way he might have looked ten or fifteen years before. He dropped his hands to his side and his face was old again. By the time the next bus came along he was shivering with the wet, and with nervousness.

He got off the bus in the center of town, crossed a small park, and went toward a restaurant which had a red and white canopy over the entrance. There was a potted plant on either side of the grilled door and a doorman in front of it with an umbrella. He saw Dalton but did not think he was a customer. He looked across the street to the park.

The door closed behind Dalton with a pneumatic swish. He stood in the foyer for a moment and then approached the wide steps that went down into the dining room. The hatcheck girl saw the old man but did not think he was a customer. She put down her nail file and leaned over the counter to see what the maitre d'hotel would do.

Dalton was stopped before he reached the steps. The maitre was sure that he was not a customer.

"Good afternoon," the maitre d'hotel said. He went no further, waiting for Dalton to explain himself.

"Good afternoon," Dalton said. He nodded with a vague smile and tried to look into the dining room.

"Have you a reservation?" asked the man.

"I'm meeting someone. Could I just take a look, and . . ."

"Does your party have a reservation?"

Dalton had to step back because the man had not moved out of the way.

"I don't know. I don't think so." Dalton tried smiling again to cover his nervousness, but it did not help. "Could I just— Would you let me look? It's important I meet him. I have to meet him—"

The maitre d'hotel stepped aside unexpectedly. He even smiled, very briefly, and nodded. "Of course, sir. Follow me." Dalton followed him into the dining room.

"Do you see your party?"

Dalton looked carefully, and then shook his head. He was holding his lower lip in his teeth to keep himself from making a sound.

"Perhaps your party has left? Perhaps you had in mind a similar restaurant, further down the street?"

"No. No, it was here. I'm late. I knew I'd be late." Dalton sounded as if he were talking to himself.

The maitre d'hotel stood there for a moment, and then shrugged.

"I'm sorry. Did you wish to order, in the meantime?"

"Look," said Dalton. He had not been listening. "He must have been here. Or maybe he'll come back, because . . ."

"What is the name of your party? Can you describe him?"

Dalton looked around again and unbuttoned his overcoat. He felt damp and warm. He saw how the maitre d'hotel looked at the overcoat, and then turned to the stairs. Dalton had to follow or the maitre d'hotel would not have heard him.

"A young man—hard to describe. He wears dark clothes, a dark suit most of the time. His face, his eyes are light, but he has black hair—" Dalton ran into the maitre d'hotel who had stopped at the top of the stairs.

"I'm sorry— I was saying—"

"I don't seem to recall such a party. Your description—" The maitre d'hotel did not finish. He was looking elsewhere.

"He might have been here," Dalton insisted. "He would have drunk coffee. He lets it sit till it gets cold and then he drinks it."

"I'm sorry."

The maitre d'hotel stepped aside. He did not offer the old man one of the seats in the foyer. He watched briefly as the old man went back to the door.

It was still raining outside, but it was only a fine mist now. Slowly, Dalton walked back the way he had come, and when he entered the park he sat down on a bench. His coat was still open. He sat and looked at his feet.

Across the street a taxi stopped at the awning. The attendant with the umbrella rushed to the cab, but he wasn't in time. And he wasn't in time to hold open the grilled door to the restaurant.

By that time the man was in the foyer. He asked the maitre d'hotel for a table and ordered coffee. He wore a dark suit and did not touch his cup until the coffee had gotten quite cold.

## *Chapter 2*

DANIEL PORT sat there for a while longer. Now and then he tapped the rim of his empty cup, looked at the foyer, and looked away again. Then he started to whistle, hardly audibly. Finally he put a bill on the table and went back to the foyer.

"I was expecting an elderly man," he said to the maitre d'hotel. "Tall, sort of, and thin. Has he been here?"

"An elderly man?"

"His name is Dalton. I was to meet . . ."

"He did not give his name. Someone like that was here about ten or fifteen minutes ago. I'm afraid he . . ."

"If he comes back, ask him to wait, will you?" Port left.

He didn't have to ask the doorman about Dalton because he saw the old man on the other side of the street, sitting in the park. Dalton was hunched over on the bench, watching the restaurant, but without the purpose which would have enabled him to make out Port.

Port ran across the street and started waving.

"Hey, Abe! Here I am! Abe!"

Then Dalton was up, smiling tremulously, and the two men shook hands.

"Abe, am I glad to see you! Jesus, I'm sorry I almost missed you. Why didn't you wait inside? Come on, man, you look like hell out here in the rain—"

Dalton looked at Port and smiled at him again. "You came," he said. "You got my note. Danny, you're looking good, very good." Then he let Port take him by the arm and guide him across the street.

"Why didn't you wait inside?" Port asked again. Sitting there like a wet cat—" He made Dalton laugh. Dalton was very glad to see Port.

"You know," he said. "The kind of a place it is, and me, the way I am—"

"Jesus, *you* picked the place. Why did you pick that kind of a place?"

They were at the door and the doorman sprang to open it for them. Port looked at the maitre d'hotel and held up two fingers. "Why this place?" he said again.

"Because—well, meeting you," Dalton said, almost whispering, "I figured maybe this is the kind of place you always go to. I been hearing how you done well and all that, and maybe this is the only kind you go to any more. You know—"

"Christ!" said Port.

They sat down, and then Dalton got up again to take off his overcoat. The waiter took it back to the checkroom.

"Whatever you got to say, I'm not listening, Abe," Port said. "Not till you eat." Dalton ordered some soup and a pudding and he ate while Port sat over a fresh cup of coffee and smoked.

"How long you been out, Abe?" he asked after a while.

"Almost a month," said Dalton. He put down his spoon and said, "Look, Danny. The reason . . ."

"Eat." Dalton ate and Port said, "Didn't you get fifteen?"

Dalton nodded and said, "Good behavior." The waiter came back to ask if there'd be anything else.

"Something to drink," said Port. "Coffee, Abe?"

Dalton shook his head and ordered milk. When the waiter had gone he said, "And for health. They let me out, considering my health." The milk came and he started to sip it. "I was costing too much."

"You lost a lot of weight," said Port. "You couldn't have cost much on the food bill."

Dalton put his hand on the table and looked at the bony knuckles.

"No stomach," he said. "They took out seven eighths of the stomach." Dalton put down his glass with a sudden clunk. He looked at Port and smiled. "So tell me, Danny. Is it true what I hear? About you and the Stoker outfit?"

"I don't know what you heard," said Port, "but Stoker died and I quit the racket."

"That's what I heard," said Dalton. He kept looking at Port and started shaking his head. "Imagine," he said. "Imagine. Ten years ago, just a kid, almost . . ."

"I was no kid," said Port.

"No." Dalton laughed shortly. "Not the way you were starting to climb. You and Stoker sure got along, didn't you?"

"He tried to teach me, yes."

Dalton leaned over the table and said, "So how come you quit, Danny?"

"Stoker died."

"You could have taken over. How come?"

Port gestured to the waiter to bring him more coffee.

"I hear you left clean, Danny. Why?"

Port moved his mouth as if he meant to whistle, and then he said, "I had mine. There're some people I wouldn't work with."

"But last time I saw you . . ."

"I was ten years younger."

Port watched the waiter put down the coffee and then he said, "You and me had quite a time there, for a while, huh, Abe?" He smiled at the old man.

"I remember. When I asked Stoker about pulling that job in his territory, you told him he shouldn't let me."

"Stoker never was a jug heavy. He ran a political territory, and for you to knock over a bank in a hot ward like his meant nothing but trouble."

"Yes," said Dalton. He sipped his milk again. "I got caught. I was getting old." They were both silent for a moment. "Anyway, Danny, you were real good to me afterwards. Trying to help with the law, and in prison."

Port said, "I got respect for a man with a craft." He gave Dalton's old hand a pat. "Pure art, the way you used to set up some of your jobs. As a matter of fact, Abe, I can't think of a single jug heavy today . . ."

"That's over," said Dalton. His voice was suddenly very cold with control, and Port heard the change in tone.

"How did you know I was in town?" he said.

"I asked around. I wanted to see you, Danny."

"Yes," said Port. "That's why I came."

They looked at each other and then Dalton said, "Could we go someplace else, Dan?"

Port paid the bill, and asked the doorman to call a taxi.

"My place?" he asked Dalton.

"I don't know, Dan. Maybe someplace else, maybe . . ."

"Go up ten blocks," Port told the cabby.

They got out in front of the museum and went up the stone steps. The wetness blew into their faces and the feeling of dankness did not leave them when they went inside. The hall was gray marble and the ceiling was very high. A guard looked at them and then looked away. They went into a room that recreated an early New England kitchen, with beams on the ceiling, chinked walls, a black pot hanging inside a hearth, and a wooden table covered with pewter dishes. Dalton sat down on a bench and unbuttoned his coat. He looked up at Port, then back down at his coat again. Port was at the table, touching the pewter ware. The plates had been nailed to the table boards and the utensils had been wired down. Port sat down next to Dalton.

"Did you know I'm from New England?" said Dalton.

Port shook his head.

"I'm out the last time," said Dalton. "The next time is for good."

"I know," said Port.

"I need your help."

"Of course, Abe. You need money?"

"No." Dalton's old hands started stroking each other, making drying motions.

"All right," said Port. He tried to think of something to say that would change the mood of tiredness that showed in Dalton. "Sure," he said. "You used to pick well. The Baintree job, fifteen thousand; the National job, sixty-five thousand; and all those . . ."

"I have five hundred and twenty-one dollars," said Dalton, "and I want to go home. I have a ticket for the train going east and once I get home I won't need much. A room, a small job— I have a nephew there. He once promised—" Dalton's voice trailed off. He spoke again, his voice was suddenly raw now. "I am very sick. I am not going to die in prison."

Port said nothing.

"I can't lose again," said Dalton.

"Tell me, Abe. Somebody won't let you quit?"

Dalton nodded.

"How hard is he squeezing you?"

"If I don't handle his heist, I go back to prison. He can put me there."

"How sure are you?"

"Very." Dalton laughed harshly. "I trained that kid. I used to show him the plans of jobs I did alone. I showed him so he'd learn. Jobs they never pinned on me."

"Who is he?"

"Dicky."

"I don't think I know him."

"He's changed a lot." Dalton seemed to be talking to himself. "He acts crazy—"

"He's in town?"

"Yes. Dicky Corday."

## *Chapter 3*

DICKY CORDAY lived in a hotel on the south side of town. The plaster was peeling in great strips and the wallpaper in all the rooms had large, faded flowers. None of this bothered Corday because he wasn't going to stay there much longer. First came a small burg called Newton, then Palm Springs or Hot Springs or some place like that. He whistled at himself in the mirror and pulled up his tie so that his silk collar would drape like two leaves on each side.

"You still in that shower?" he yelled suddenly, but the girl in the shower couldn't hear him because of the water.

"Letty!"

She heard him that time. She turned off the water and in her haste got a cold spray down her back that made her gasp.

"What now?"

"Nothing," she said. "Nothing, Dicky."

"Don't gimme that nothing! I just heard you say something in there and I wanna know what it was!"

"Dicky, please. All it was I got cold water down over my back and all I did was make a sound."

He started cursing her for being a lamebrain and more stupid than anyone ought to be. His voice frightened her and she wrapped a towel around her and then rubbed her head so she couldn't hear what he said. But she heard him yelling again.

"—coming outa there pretty soon?"

"I'm drying myself, Dicky. Please, don't be yelling at me all the time."

"Drying yourself? Come outa there and dry yourself in here."

She sighed, held the towel so it wouldn't drag on the floor, and came out of the bathroom.

Dicky sat in the green chair with the doilies and one leg was dipping up and down over the arm rest. The girl watched his leg dipping and worried about his mood.

"Let's go," he said. "Let's see you dry yourself."

She started on her head again, holding the towel so that it wouldn't slip.

"The body, for Chrissakes! Who cares about the head!"

"But my hair . . ."

"Just drop it," he said. "Drop the towel."

She dropped the towel and stood there while he looked. She lowered her head to see her feet, trying to keep herself from feeling embarrassed, but then she saw her breasts.

"You're blushing," said Dicky and he roared with laughter. "An old pro like you, and blushing."

She wasn't old and she was no pro, and the situation she found herself in now wasn't anything new. It was his look, she thought, his look would make her blush even with clothes on.

"Okay," he said. "Start drying."

She dried herself and Dicky watched. He sat sprawled in the chair and he laughed when she looked awkward.

She was shaped beautifully. Her skin was very white and her slight plumpness gave her soft shadows. She looked all soft. The same quality, in her face, gave her a look of something unfinished. She seemed to have just awakened.

"Come here," he said. "Drop that damn towel and come here."

"But I'm not dry yet, Dicky. I got to . . ."

"Why don't you shut up that mouth?" he said and started cursing again. He yanked her down by one arm, and when she had fallen across the chair he grabbed her hard around her back, dug his face into her neck, and bit her. She struggled, afraid to struggle too much, and gasped, afraid to scream. When he let her go she sat up. She looked at him and made herself smile because he was grinning at her.

"Like that, huh?" He gave her a slap.

She got up and said, "I want to get dressed now, Dicky, so we can . . ."

"You liked that, huh?"

"Yes, Dicky."

"What are you lying for, you stupid dame! Huh? Answer me!"

"Dicky, please—"

"Answer me!"

"I—I don't know what to say, honest, Dicky—"

"Did you like it?"

"I don't know— It hurt—"

"So why don't you say so?" He went to the mirror and retied his tie. "Get dressed," he said over his shoulder. "He ought to get here just about now."

Letty started to dress in the corner by the bed and Dicky watched her in the mirror.

"You didn't answer me when I asked you."

She stopped what she was doing and said, "Asked me what, Dicky? I don't remember."

"Why you didn't say so. Why you didn't say it hurt?"

She finished hooking her bra and didn't know what to answer.

"Well?" He sounded mean.

"Because—because I was afraid—"

He laughed loudly, but he said nothing else. Then he saw her put her arms into the slip and lift it up over her head.

"Hey, Letty."

She stopped and looked at him.

"I got this idea. Leave it off."

She looked at him without understanding. "But your friend is coming, this old man."

"That's why," said Dicky. "Make him all fidgety and embarrassed."

"No," said Letty.

"What did you say?"

She put on her slip. "No," she said again.

Dicky stared at her for a moment, watched her put on her dress, and then he started to laugh again. He got a bottle out of the closet and put it and a glass on the table. He poured himself a drink and then lit a cigarette. He said nothing else to the girl. Sometimes, when a certain tone came into her voice, he left her alone.

He drank for a while and watched Letty make up the bed and then he went to the window and looked out into the street. He couldn't see much, because of the fire escape in front, and because it was night and there were few lights on the street. He watched the hotel sign below his window. It had a border of blinking bulbs and Dicky held his breath to see how many blinks he could last.

"Is he going to the dance with us?" said Letty. "The old man that's coming?"

He let out his breath, making Letty start.

"Hell, no," he said. He went back to the table and when he passed Letty he slapped her behind. "Dalton won't stay long," he said. "One way or the other, there's just going to be one or two words spoken between us."

"About the job?"

"His job," said Dicky and suddenly he looked very

cheerful. "How come you're wearing that deadbeat rag? Put on something with color, something that shines, Letty. Something that shines!" When she walked past him he gave her another slap on the rump.

He watched her change and then said, "Now some perfume, honey. Something that makes their eyes water, Letty." It sounded so good to him he started laughing again. "And when I'm through with old Dalton . . ."

"Dicky," she said. "Stop drinking so much."

"I can't drink in my own place? Who in hell . . ."

"Dicky, I think I hear somebody coming."

"That's old reliable," Dicky said. He sat down in his chair, crossed one leg over the other and started to dip it. He gave a hoist to his tie and grinned. "Smile, honey," he said. "Here comes our future."

"If you want me to leave, Dicky . . ."

"Naw, stay. Just go over there and open that door. Open that door with a big shiny grin, and when . . ."

There was a knock.

"Open the door, lamebrain! Don't you hear?"

Letty ran to open the door, catching some of Dicky's excitement. She fumbled it open, smiling the way she was told.

"Yes sir!" yelled Dicky. "Dalton rides again, huh, Dalton?" and he waved at the old man to come in. "And as soon as Letty gets the door shut tight— The door, lamebrain! Close that . . ."

Port came in and closed the door himself.

He came into the room and nobody said anything. Letty had nothing to say, Dalton was very nervous, and Dicky wasn't sure of the situation yet.

"What gives?" he said. "You know this guy, Dalton?"

The old man cleared his throat but Dicky didn't wait to hear.

"You bring this guy, Dalton? What is this, huh? You trying to . . ."

"I brought my friend," Dalton began. Then Dicky got up, pushed Dalton out of the way so that the old man staggered, and stepped up close to Port.

"Who are you?" he said, making it sound like an insult.

"My name's Port. Daniel Port. I'm a friend of Abe Dalton's and he asked me to come along."

"Why? You muscling in on this deal?"

"What deal?" said Port.

The question made Dicky frown and quickly he looked from one man to the other. Then he swiveled around fast and shouted at Dalton. "You got something in mind we wasn't planning? You come up here, maybe, to try . . ."

"If you'll stop shouting," Dalton said very clearly, "I'll explain this to you."

The voice was a surprise. It seemed calm suddenly, and Dalton was no longer the way he should be—old, scared, and too tired to kick.

"It's about this heist you want me to handle. I won't lie to you, Dicky, and say that I want to do it, and you know that I'm much too old to start double-crossing anyone now. So I won't say that I'm going through with it and then pull some trick to get out. But I brought my friend—" Dalton pointed—"and he thought, with him sitting in, maybe we can work something out. You see, Dicky . . ."

"Who is this guy? Cop?"

Dalton frowned, and Letty put in, "He just said, Dicky—he wouldn't double-cross."

She saw Dicky react and was sorry she had opened her mouth.

"I'm not the police," Port said, "and if you weren't such a stupid jerk I'd try explaining it to you, about Dalton, and what he's up against with this squeeze play you put him into. But I'll tell you this much, Corday—"

Port stopped when he saw the color change in Dicky's face. There was no point in talking to a man who was boiling with rage.

"Who is this?" said Dicky. "Who is this big shot?"

"He used to be with Stoker," said Dalton. "You remember the Stoker outfit?"

"A big shot—"

"He and Stoker were close," Dalton went on, but he didn't get any further.

"Big shot," Dicky said again, "trying to queer my setup, huh?" For a moment he didn't seem to know what to do next. Then he said, "I don't need no big shot the way I'm gonna run this." He grabbed Letty's arm and dragged her to the door.

"Dicky," said Dalton. "Wait. We haven't—"

"Go jump," said Dicky, and tore open the door. "I'm going dancing."

He saw Dalton's face change with surprise and before he banged the door behind him he started roaring with laughter. Port and Dalton could hear him laughing all the way down the stairs.

## *Chapter 4*

IT TOOK Port a while to calm the old man.

"Danny," Dalton said when Dicky had left, "If he goes ahead now—"

"Don't get the shakes, Abe. He won't do a thing."

"You saw how crazy he is, Dan. You saw you can't tell what he'll do next."

"He's not so crazy as to send you back to jail and lose out on this deal he has in mind. All he knows now . . ."

"If he goes ahead, Dan—if he goes ahead— The old man ended by shaking his head and sinking into a chair. He sat there, shaking his head and looking at the floor.

Port didn't say anything for a while. He went to the window and stood there, staring out. After a while he started to whistle, making a slow, tuneless sound.

"Dalton," he said. When he heard the old man sit up Port said, "If you just wait and do nothing you'll go back to prison for sure."

Dalton got up and Port turned to face him. There was real fear in the old man's face. His mouth started to work and he moved his hands in helpless gestures. When his voice came it was high, like a wail.

"Do you know what it's like? Do you know what it's like to sit on that rock remembering what it's like outside, and then trying harder and harder all the time to remember because you've begun to forget, and the worst thing of all when you start caring less and less and you think maybe it isn't so bad to sit inside a hole made out of concrete with the sky sliced up in the same black angles day after day! That's what it's like! And I'm not going to die that way!"

He was finished and breathing hard, and when he sat down on the chair again it was because he was tired. He looked at his hands and said, "I don't know. I don't know if you see it." And then, very low, "But I mean it."

Port sat down too. He played with a cigarette for a while, as if nothing else interested him. Then he said, "Where does Dicky go dancing?"

"Dancing?" said Dalton. He shrugged. "I don't know. Maybe Nick's—Nick's Palace—or the Off-Time."

"That's in the neighborhood?"

"Yeah," said Dalton. "He likes to hang around with his punk friends." He coughed. "Look, Danny. I've thought this over. I think the best thing is to go through with it. It's a risk either way—doing the job with Dicky or not doing the job—but maybe I got more of a chance if I do that heist."

"Don't be a fool," said Port.

"No, I mean it. There's a small toolmaking plant in this town, Newton, and the way I hear it the job isn't so bad."

"Dalton, you haven't even let me try to help you. I haven't even . . ."

Dalton went on as if he hadn't heard. "Their payroll is big—toolmakers' and diemakers' wages, that kind of thing—and it's one of the few places that still pays in cash."

"Listen to me, Abe—"

"The money goes to the plant Thursday night and lies there till pay time, Friday. Hell," Dalton said, "when I think of some of the jobs I pulled . . ."

"You forgetting the time you did for it?" said Port.

Dalton looked at Port, then away.

"And forgetting the crazy type you're going to be working with? I wouldn't even go stealing apples with that screwball punk. I'd be afraid he might not like the tone of my voice and start arguing manners with me, right there with the apples in his hands and pockets."

"I don't know," Dalton said, "I can't even think—"

"Listen to me," said Port.

Dalton sat and listened. It was the easiest thing to do.

"You're going home now. Go to bed and do nothing. Just sleep. I'll get to you by tomorrow noon and maybe we'll know more."

"What?" said Dalton. He did not seem to expect much of an answer.

"I don't know yet," said Port. He got up and tossed away the cigarette he had been mangling on the top of the table. "But know this, Abe. You won't have to pull that heist."

They left together. Dalton told Port where he lived and where Dicky might be. Then Dalton went one way and Port went the other.

It had stopped raining. There were shiny black puddles in the empty street and the night air was wet. Port walked down the empty tenement streets. He could see a white curtain flapping out of a window high up and sometimes the slow waving of sheets hanging in the dark shaft of a yard. He walked, smoking a cigarette and wishing for a cup of coffee. He did not know yet what he would do about Dalton and Dicky Corday.

Nick's Palace was a small, dark place crowded with a bar, booths, and a bandstand. A hard-looking female in dungarees was playing a steel guitar, singing mountain songs in a Hawaiian beat. The dance floor was crowded with working people and neighborhood punks. Port remembered that Dicky wasn't much taller than the girl Letty, and he tried spotting the couple that way. He might have done better had Dicky been tall, because everyone else seemed to be. Port looked in the booths, remembering that Letty had sandy brown hair, but there were many brown-haired women around, none of them Letty.

"You been staring at her long enough," somebody said, and when Port looked down the man in the booth took the toothpick out of his mouth and said, "You just looking, or buying?"

Port didn't know immediately what the man meant.

"You want her, or don't you?" The man thumbed at the girl sitting next to him.

"No," said Port. "I was looking for someone else," and he tried squeezing by the booth.

But the man had gotten up and he was in the way now, his face close to Port's. The man whispered, "She's all right. Low rates, too." Then he stepped aside to let the woman get out of the booth.

She was old. She was thin and old, the make-up she wore fixing a weird mask of youth on her face.

"Let's dance," she said to Port and put one arm over his shoulder. Past Port's ear she called, "A tango, Melissa!" at the woman who played the guitar.

The dungareed woman played a mountain song in tango tempo and the made-up face was close to Port's.

"Come on," she said. "I love dancing."

"I don't tango," said Port. "I was looking for someone else. I didn't mean . . ."

"That's all right. Just move your hips."

"Look," said Port, "I don't mean to offend you . . ."

"That's all right." She stood close, because of the crush on the floor. Then she said without any banter, "Can't you just dance with me?"

"Sure," said Port.

"Just dance. No obligations."

Port held her around the waist and they danced.

She smelled of talcum powder. She moved with the rhythm and hummed the beat to herself. She said nothing else.

After a while Port said, "You really do like to dance, don't you?"

"Nothing but." She smiled at him. "I was going to be a dancer."

When the number was over she didn't give Port a chance. She said, "One more, huh? I don't get to dance much around here."

"I'm really sorry, but I told you I'm looking . . ."

"Come on, just one more. Maybe I can help." She laughed humorlessly. "I know everybody around here."

The dungareed woman started another song, and they danced again.

"You know somebody called Dicky Corday?" Port said into her ear.

"That nothing? Sure. What about him?"

"I'm looking for him. He went dancing tonight and I thought he might be here."

"He was," said the woman, "but Letty don't like it here."

"I didn't think Dicky was the type who listened to anyone."

"He does, to Letty. I seen her grow up. That kid, she'll do just about anything, but now and then—all of a sudden it comes—she says no."

"I wouldn't have thought Dicky'd take that sort of thing."

"He does, though," said the woman.

"Where did they go from here?" Port wanted to know.

"The Off-Time, I guess." And like an afterthought, "That Letty sure likes to dance."

"Dicky too?"

"He don't care. It's Letty. I used to know her mother," said the woman. "She was the same way."

"And her father?"

"Father. She's got a million of 'em, for all I know."

The set was over and the woman, without being asked, let go of Port and pushed her way back to the booth. Port had to hurry and lean close to her in order to make her hear him.

"Thank you for the dance," he told her. "I think you're good."

She started to smile, but then she stopped herself. She sounded off-hand.

"The floor's too small. You can't really do nothing here."

"It was nice, though," said Port and then he nodded good-by.

"You'll be around again, maybe?" she said at the last moment.

"If I'm still in the neighborhood, I'll be back," said Port.

She smiled and then he turned away. He remembered, going out of the door, that she had not told him her name, and that she had not asked him his.

## *Chapter 5*

THE OFF-TIME was a roller-skating rink, but twice a week—on Tuesdays and Fridays—the management hired a combo of five and turned the rink into a dance floor. Bright lights glared over the rink but there were very few lights on the other side of the railing, where the tables were. There were setups on the tables and the men kept their bottles under the chairs. The women all looked alike. They giggled too much and wore the wrong kind of jewelry.

When Port had walked half the length of the railing toward the bandstand he saw Dicky and the girl. They were dancing close to the rail because Dicky was talking to someone. Letty danced with eyes closed, humming, waiting for Dicky to finish talking. The man who was talking across the rail looked like a delinquent grown-up. Dicky was telling him a joke.

He stopped talking suddenly. He stopped dancing, too. Letty opened her eyes, and Dicky's buddy, who had been ready with his laugh through the whole long story, put a cigarette in his mouth and took one nervous puff.

"Come on, man, don't stop now! What she say when . . ."

"*You!* Who in hell sent for you!"

Dicky's buddy cut loose with a loud haw-haw that shook him all over. He turned it off as quickly.

"What's the matter, there's more?"

Then he caught his mistake. He followed Dicky's eyes and saw the man Dicky was staring at. He didn't know Port, but he disliked him immediately. He didn't like the smile on Port's face, the way he was leaning against the rail, the suit he had on, the way his hair was cut.

"This square bothering you, Dicky?"

Dicky curled his mouth and said, "Ha!"

"You say the word, Dicky?"

"It's hard to tell," Port cut in. "He's the strong, grunty kind." Port smiled.

Dicky's buddy looked from one man to the other, wiped the backs of his hands as if stroking boxing gloves tight over the knuckles, and took a swift step forward. It looked very dramatic, but it ended right there.

He stiffened all over, and color spread all over his face from the effort to keep the scream out of his throat. Then air hissed through his clenched teeth as he slowly bent over and took hold of his knee.

Port's foot tapping into the man's shin had made only a small, wooden sound. The man limped to the nearest chair, still in slow motion, his breath a tight wheeze.

"I'm sorry," said Port, and looked at Dicky, "but I didn't come to see him."

"Yeah," Dicky said. For the moment he couldn't say anything else.

"I came to see you."

"Yeah."

"You and Letty ran out so fast I couldn't get a word in edgewise."

"Yeah."

Port cocked his head to one side and looked at Dicky. "Something bothering you?" He looked at Letty. "Or is he like this often?"

Letty didn't know what to say. She had no talent for banter but she knew it was foolish to answer Port seriously.

"You got troubles," said Dicky and he gave his voice a raw, ominous tone. He said the same thing again the same way, and it seemed to loosen him up. "Port, wasn't it?" He moved up to the railing. Letty followed him.

"Dan," said Port. "Might as well, since we'll be knowing each other much better before we're through."

"Before me and you are through," Dicky started but he stopped when he saw Port frown.

"Look," said Port, "It's no fun horsing around with you. Let's try it serious."

"You wanna step outside?" Dicky said. "Right now?"

"The hell with that." Port looked annoyed. "All I want is one brief word with you and you can go back to your dancing." He smiled at Letty when he said the last. "I just came to tell you . . ."

"You wanna go outside right now?" Dicky said again.

Port took a deep breath. He was sorry he had come to this place. He should have known that Dicky would show off in front of his girl, that he still would be sore at Dalton for bringing Port, and—maybe worst of all—that Dicky would be on home ground here.

Dicky's friend was no longer alone. He was still on the chair, leg bent and body crouched over, but now three punks in black-and-white satin jackets were standing by like an honor guard. The longer the injured punk crouched there the more fiercely the others looked around.

"No," said Port, "I don't want to go outside with you. All I want is to make an appointment with you. You, me, and Dalton. We can . . ."

"Who needs you?" said Dicky.

"Dalton does. You shouldn't push an old man like that. Your place, ten tomorrow. How's that?"

Dicky didn't answer.

"We don't have to make a production of this. How about it, Corday? Ten tomorrow?"

"Get out of my way," said Dicky. He was looking past Port. "You injured my buddy."

Port felt like smiling at Corday's choice of words, but when he saw Dicky start climbing over the railing he changed his mind.

"Letty," he said. "Can't you talk to him? All I'm asking . . ."

"You shut up," Dicky said to the girl.

"You going to leave Letty standing around here?" said Port.

Dicky pushed him out of the way and Port let him go. There were now five punks by the chair, not counting the sufferer, and all of them waiting for Dicky Corday. Port turned his back and swung his legs over the railing. Letty just stood there. And then Port had his hand on her arm.

"My pleasure," he said and danced the girl off toward the middle of the rink. He could see the tough boys all standing in the dark on the other side of the railing, their hands in their pockets, smoking the way Humphrey Bogart might.

Port thought he might have enjoyed dancing with Letty if he had met her some other way. Now he held the girl lightly, giving her plenty of room, and thought of other things. This was his night for dancing, all right.

"Letty," he said, "how long have you been with Corday?"

"Oh!" she said, disappointed, when the music stopped. She looked up at Port. "The set isn't over—"

He nodded and said, "Fine. We'll stay out here."

She moved back into position.

"Letty," he began again, but Letty said "Shh!" and waited for Port to move on the right beat because the music was playing again.

They danced to a slow, heavy rhythm, Letty with her eyes closed and Port looking up at the ceiling. The structural steel had been left open and paper garlands—

red, white, and green—were wound around I-beams and struts.

"To do it right," said Letty, "you got to hold me closer." Then she moved closer to him and pushed his right hand lower on her back. She hitched her torso around so that they would fit properly.

"And you got to move more than just with the legs," she said, "or it isn't dancing."

She spoke very seriously and when she was satisfied with their position she kept still again and just danced.

"Better this way?" said Port.

"That's fine. Keep your steps short and smooth. You're doing fine now. It's different from walking."

Port sighed. "Does Dicky do this well?" he asked. He had to start somewhere.

"He's all right."

She started to hum.

"You known him long?"

"Hm-hm," she said.

Port chewed his lip. He looked up at the ceiling again, at the paper frills wound around the steel beams and at the dust up there. He started to feel very useless.

"You got to—to think you're in a wave, you know," Letty said. "And the music is the wave."

"Yes," said Port. "I'll try it."

"That's what I think of," she said and closed her eyes again.

It improved Port's dancing, but did not make him feel any better. "Letty," he said. "The reason I'm out here with you's got nothing to do with dancing." He waited a moment, but she said nothing. "I want to ask about Dicky."

"I don't care," she said. She started to hum again.

"You like Dicky?" Port asked her.

"Sure."

"He like you?"

She nodded, humming.

"I'm asking because he doesn't seem to like too many people."

"He doesn't like you," she said.

"You know why?" said Port.

"You're butting in," she said. "He doesn't like that."

"He's butting in on that old man, Dalton."

"That's because Dalton's a doublecrosser."

"What? Dalton?"

"That's what Dicky says."

"You've got that wrong, Letty."

"That's what Dicky says," she repeated and then the music stopped and the sax trailed off and the piece was over.

"There's one more in the set," Letty said. She stepped back, pulled her dress smooth in front, and waited.

Port nodded. He and Letty stood near the bandstand. He looked over at the darkened area where the tables were. It was not easy to see well, but Port saw that the table where the punks had been was empty. The black-and-white jackets were posted at regular intervals, one at each gate in the railing, two at the main exit, one each where a red bulb glowed over the side exits into the alley-way.

"The last one in a set is the longest," said Letty. "You know how to jitterbug?"

Port had started to whistle tunelessly.

"You know how to jitterbug?"

"We'll just dance," said Port. "Like before."

"You can let me go a few times, can't you? You just hold one hand, this hand here, and keep up the beat. Then I come back."

The music started with a crash from the bandstand, and then, without pause, went into a quick, nervous riff.

Port held Letty close.

"What's this doublecross Dalton pulled?"

"I can't hear you," said Letty .

She tried a breakaway but Port held on. He moved her away from the bandstand.

"What did Dalton do?"

"Listen, let's try . . ."

"You listen to me," said Port. "You know why I came here. Maybe you don't think it's important." He let go of her on the beat and pushed her left hip to show her which way to spin. She shot out, smiling, and at the right time made a full twist and came back like a whip. Port caught her so that she had to face toward the railing.

"See that gate? And that one, and that one? And the exits?" She looked where he told her, keeping the beat with the slightest movement. "That's for me," said Port. "That's how important it is."

He spun her around again and she came closer. She shifted her torso for the proper fit and danced close to him.

"What happened?" she said near his ear. "Why this?"

"I'm bothering Dicky," said Port. "Now what about Dalton?"

"Dicky says Dalton promised him—that the old man was gonna set him up right, the way Dalton himself used to do."

"When was that?"

"Before prison, he says, before that last time they worked together."

"Was that the heist that put Dalton away?"

"Before then. They used to work together, now and then. I didn't know Dicky then, but he told me."

"Listen," said Port. "There's no doublecross. All you told me is Dalton was going to show Dicky the ropes and then Dalton gets caught. And for the ten years he's on the rock he gets closer and closer to dying. He's sick, he's not the same any more, and what Dicky is doing is twisting an old man who's no good any more except to rest, who's got to stop running. There's nothing Dicky can learn any more, because Dalton is through."

She looked at Port when he finished, thinking about it.

"Tell that to Dicky. Tell him the way I said it."

"I should?" she said.

"Do that. I can't get him to stand still long enough—"

"That's how he wanted it," Letty said. "That's what he told me when we left the room. He was going to keep out of your way till you left, and then he and Dalton . . ."

"What made him think I was going to leave?"

"He wasn't going to do anything. Not till you left. He told me you used to be somebody; he remembered, after a while you were somebody big in a different town—not this one."

She had said one important thing. Dicky Corday wasn't going to rush it. He wasn't going to sing the old man back into prison. He was going to bide his time, wait until Port went away, until the old man couldn't stand the threat any longer.

The five men in the combo were standing up now, whipping their bodies back and forth with the beat. The drummer was flying all over the traps and cracking the cymbals because this was the end of the number and also of the set.

"Tell him, Letty, the way I explained it," said Port, and they made a turn close to the railing.

"And then you'll leave?"

The noise was too much to be sure about Letty's voice, but Port thought she had sounded concerned; for the first time she had sounded involved.

"Why?" he asked, his head close to hers.

"It bothers Dicky," she said.

"You love him?" asked Port, but it seemed she was no longer interested in talking. She was lost in the music which was getting sharper and sharper.

When Port caught her eye he asked her again. "Why do you stay with him?"

She heard him that time. She looked as if Port had interrupted something important.

"Stay with him? Because he loves me." She said it as if it were obvious.

At the end of the swing Port let her hand go and when she saw what he was doing she stopped dancing and stood there.

"You going?"

Port swung over the railing and waved "I'm going to try hard as hell," he said. He didn't think she had heard him.

## *Chapter 6*

PORT headed for the nearest exit guarded by only one man. The band stopped before he made it, and the sudden quiet was unearthly. After the silence there was bedlam again; chairs scraped, people laughed, and a buzz of voices rose from the tables.

The kid at the door saw Port coming, but he didn't expect much from a man running away.

Then the kid's arm was suddenly bent double. The pain

grew like a fire running up his arm and bursting hot and big in his shoulder.

"It hurts less if you walk," said Port's voice close beside him, and they moved out of the door and into the alley.

One wall of the alley was dirty bricks and Port, holding the kid before him, leaned against that. The other wall was stacked high with crates. One end of the alley was blind, the other led to the street.

They stood there in the mouth of the alley, five of the black-and-white jackets.

Next to Port the exit door of the dance hall opened slowly. Holding the kid in front of him Port moved back to the blind end of the alley. He did not want anyone behind him.

Dicky Corday came into the alley accompanied by one of the jackets. They closed the door and stood by the wall, getting used to the darkness. They looked back and forth, to the dark end where Port was and to the open end where the five jackets stood.

"Tim," said Dicky Corday. "You with that bastard?"

Tim was afraid to speak because of the way Port was holding his arm.

"He got a gun on you, Tim?"

Tim didn't answer.

The nervousness started to show in Corday's voice.

"Port? I can see you. You gonna stay there and wait forever?"

Port didn't move.

"There's seven of us, Port. You needn't try to be a hero."

The silence got so bad, that suddenly Corday giggled.

The men in the jackets waited, making no move, so that Dicky couldn't delay any longer.

"Port!" he yelled. "You yellow bastard!"

Port moved, but only because Corday, to save face, wouldn't be able to delay much longer.

Pushing the kid ahead of him, Port went close to the pile of crates.

Corday heard them. "Move in," he said. "Move in, men."

"Has he got a gun, Dicky?" one of them asked.

Dicky could risk his honor no longer. "That won't

help him," he said and walked straight toward Port.

Port gave a twist to the arm he was holding and Tim's sudden scream stopped Corday. Then Corday laughed unpleasantly.

"He don't have no gun! He's holding Tim! I can see 'em!" The rest closed in fast now.

"Stay there!" said Port. They all stopped, straining to see him in the dark. "And watch this."

Port came forward, pushing Tim, and they saw how Tim was bent over.

"What's going to happen to him is . . ."

"A talker," said Dicky, because he couldn't let Port go on. "A big talker and a shin kicker we got here. Wadjasay, Jerry?" He turned to the man Port had hurt. "You gonna let the shin kicker do it again?"

Jerry moved up, swinging a slat.

"Not the shin, this time," said Port. "Worse."

"You think you can do it twice?" Dicky said. "You think it's gonna impress twice in a row?"

"It'll hurt just as much," said Port. "Twice as much, really."

Jerry felt that with everyone looking he had the most at stake. "Feller," he said, and the anger made his voice raw. "You hiding behind my buddy there. You coming out?"

"Go take a jump," said Port.

"You gonna come out, feller? You and me, huh? Just you and me—" Jerry started to crouch.

Port knew better. He said, "How about it, Dicky? Whose fight is this? His or yours?" Jerry threw the slat. It made a sharp, vicious sound as it cartwheeled through the air and then clattered along the brick wall.

They didn't hear it fall. Port had kicked at the nearest crate, so that it had started to lean very slowly into the alley where Corday and his helpers were standing. They backed up a foot at a time.

It seemed to be happening very slowly. Nor was the sound of the falling crates loud—just a brittle bouncing and some snapping sounds and then there was stillness in the alley again. If Port had let go of Tim he might have gotten away, around the crates strewn all over and the six men flush against the opposite wall.

But he thought he should drag the man along with

him, at least to the mouth of the alley. He started to move fast, but Tim didn't, and the boy's scream broke the spell. The men charged, all at once, and only the litter of crates slowed the rush.

"Corday!" called Port. He was breathing hard. "Do they know why you're pulling this? Do they know what they're helping you with?"

"Shut up, talker. You shut up and let's see . . ."

"You should tell 'em," said Port, talking fast now, "so they know how big this deal is—beating me up and getting me out of your hair. Did you tell 'em how much of a cut they'll get out of this caper?"

"I'll kill ya," Corday said. "So help me, I'll kill ya—"

"Or do they just get paid by that big feel of victory, huh? That big feel of seven guys beating up one—" But Port had said it too late and anyway the kick at Jerry had been an insult. The stalemated waiting had been an insult, the crate flying out and the pile falling over and Tim still bent over and groaning with pain was a sin and an insult.

"This was just gonna be sport," Corday was saying. "Till now, this was just gonna be . . ."

"Get this," Port interrupted, and his sudden anger made him talk through his teeth. "Call off your monkeys and beat it, or Tim pays for your trick."

"Crap," said Corday. He came closer, grinning. The jackets were following him. "Crap," said Corday. "You couldn't even . . ."

"I'll break his arm," said Port. "Watch it."

Corday laughed loudly but then he stopped.

Tim screamed.

For a moment they thought about Tim, but then they thought about insults again.

Corday stood up straight and looked around at the jackets. His grin was crazy, and his low voice was crazier still.

"Go ahead," he said. "Let's see it."

His followers stood around like curious cattle.

Port moved quickly and disjointed Tim's arm.

They were still looking at Tim writhe on the ground when Port broke Dicky's front teeth. He knew, with the next punch, that Dicky was going to double up and vomit. But Port didn't see it happen.

## *Chapter 7*

Dalton had a bed in his room, a hotplate, and a small chest of drawers. Because of the size of the room the chest stood in front of the window and the backboard cut off the light. The wallpaper was brown with a motif of fall leaves and sepia shepherd scenes.

At five in the morning Dalton lay on his back, his eyes moving along the leaves where they curled and repeated themselves. He then looked at the shepherd scenes, one after the other, to find out if there were any differences. He did this until six when he got up. Between six and seven he washed, cooked gruel on the hotplate by the window, and then went to the washroom at the end of the hall to rinse off his plate, his spoon, and the pot.

He got dressed then, not knowing what else to do. By leaning over the dresser he could bend far enough out of the window to see the clock at the corner. It was only half an hour past seven. Port had said, "I'll see you by noon."

At eight Dalton thought about smoking a cigarette. Every day, since he had had to stop smoking, he had thought about having a cigarette at eight in the morning. By now he was able to say to himself that thinking of smoking was a keener pleasure than doing the real thing.

After this he cleaned his room and brushed his suit and overcoat. Then he sat on his bed and looked at his hands. He used to take very good care of his hands. He used to keep them very clean, the nails very short, and use salves and ointments to make the skin very supple at the fingertips. At one time he had always worn gloves. It had been his trademark. Gloves Dalton. He didn't know if the gloves kept his fingers more sensitive, but he had read about Arséne Lupin or some such French gentleman-thief and he had always felt elegant wearing gray gloves.

He touched the tips of his fingers now They felt cold. His fingers looked like pale roots, just taken out of frozen ground.

It was barely past nine.

Dalton took a full, slow breath but had to stop in the middle. The deep pressure made the ache in his stomach a boring, hot rasp. He did not reach for the bottle of milk because he knew it would make him feel bloated. He might even get sick. He lay down on the bed holding very still so that his clothes would not wrinkle. He closed his eyes and imagined how it might be without the pain in his middle.

Then the pain was gone. He woke with a start that shook the bed. His pants legs slid up over his calves when he rushed to get his feet to the floor. The window. The street was bright with a high sun. The clock, at the corner, said one-thirty-five.

Dalton swallowed. Look again, slowly, he thought. The clock said one-thirty-six now.

If Port had been here, knocking, waiting, and he, Dalton, had slept . . . Port had not come. Of course not. And if Port had not come it was worse.

The old man began to tremble. He sat down. He rubbed his mouth and the loose skin under his jaw. He could not afford to think about Port, to wonder about him, while Dicky—Dalton jumped up from the bed and tore his overcoat off the hook. Dicky Corday was crazy; he might do anything. Port had threatened him, maybe. To threaten Dicky Corday, crazy with glory dreams— Dalton ran down the street, not daring to look up at the clock again. He wished he had not taken the overcoat. The coat made him hot, slowed him down. Dicky lived far away for an old man, for the pain running made in the throat and in his legs. . . .

## *Chapter 8*

At first there was no answer when Dalton knocked on the hotel-room door. He knocked once more, and this time he heard a sound. He could not make it out at first, but then he heard Dicky's voice.

"Who in hell is it?"

"Me. Abe. Abe Dalton."

Dalton waited again, hearing nothing, and then Dicky started to laugh.

"Come in!" Dicky called. "The door's open."

Dalton opened the door and walked in. When he saw Dicky and the girl Dalton did not know whether to stay or to leave.

"Close the door," said Dicky. "This ain't a public place."

Dalton came into the room and sat down by the table. He sat on the edge of the chair not knowing where to look, but the bed was right opposite him, with Letty and Dicky there.

Dicky was wearing his clothes, but Letty was not. She wore a slip which covered little and when she tired to get up Dicky pushed her back on the bed. He held her down and looked over to Dalton.

"About time you showed up," he said.

Dalton noticed the lisp. There was one front tooth missing and another one was broken.

"You staring at Letty or me?" Dicky said and the grin showed the hole in his teeth. He got off the bed and sat in the chair with the doilies.

"Take a shower, and then run down and get some coffee," he said to Letty. He looked at Dalton. "What's on your mind?" he said to the old man. "Anything I should know?"

"I can come back," said Dalton. "Any time you say I should be back, Dicky, I'll . . ."

"Letty's all right," said Dicky. "Don't you think Letty's all right?"

Dalton said, "Where's Dan Port?"

The shower went on in the bathroom and Dicky looked at the door.

"Listen to this," he said without looking at Dalton, and then they heard the girl make a sound.

"Every time," said Dicky. "Every time she goes in, the water's too hot." Then he leaned back in the chair, pulled a cigar out of his shirt pocket and lit it.

"Smoke, Dalton?"

Dalton shook his head. He looked at the wall and then at the window, and tried not to look the way he was feeling.

"What's that you asked me, Dalton?"

"I asked— I wondered if you knew where Port is. You remember—"

"Oh, him! What do you want him for, Dalton?"

Dalton knew that he could not take much more. He stood up and unbuttoned his coat. He took it off, hoping it would cool him, and then he sat down again.

"You tell me about Port," he said, "and then I'm ready to talk business with you. All right, Dicky?"

Dicky nodded and put the cigar in a tray. "Kinda makes you feel rotten the way you tried pulling a trick on me yesterday, don't it, Dalton?"

"Dicky, I'm here today . . ."

"Yeah. I know. Business. What makes you think I still wanna talk to you?"

There was a pause and then Dalton said, "No," like a groan.

"Scared you huh?" Dicky got up, went to the window, and threw the cigar down to the street. He turned back to the room with his hands in his pockets and leaned on the window sill. Dicky Corday looked very strong, very agile, but at rest for the moment.

"I'm no bastard, like you think. Don't worry, Dalton. I didn't sing to the cops."

For the moment that was all Dalton wanted to know. Right then nothing more mattered. He ran his hands over his face and let the tiredness come. He felt almost grateful to Corday.

"So now that you're ready for business, Dalton—" Dicky came away from the window—"let's you and me get this done." He hauled a trunk out from under the bed, unlocked it with a key from his pocket, and took out a long roll of paper. "You got a pencil, Dalton?" But before Dalton could answer Dicky slammed the trunk lid and came back to the table. He put the rolled papers on top of the table with a vigorous slap. "Like old times, huh, Dalton?" He laughed loud and hard.

Dalton sank into his chair. He had thought that he was ready for this, knowing it had been inevitable, but there also had been a hope—not large or convincing—but a hope.

"I asked you," he said, "and you never answered, Dicky. You know what happened to Port?"

Dicky ran his tongue over his teeth and then he turned

his head to look at the bathroom door. The water was going off, and then Letty made that sound again, of breath drawn in sharply.

"What now?" he yelled. "Cold water all over your back?"

"I'm sorry, Dicky. I couldn't—"

"Lamebrain!" Dicky turned back to the table. He got out another cigar and ran the length of it back and forth under his nose. "Do I know what happened to Port?" he said. He sounded quiet and conversational. "I happened to Port." He stuck the cigar in his mouth.

"Oh," said Dalton, not knowing what else to say, and not wanting to hear any more.

"I'll tell you exactly," Dicky went on, "so you'll know." He lit his cigar and let the smoke run out of his mouth. "First of all, he comes mooching around and gives me a hard time. He wanted a cut, the way I see it. Then he don't get anywhere." Dicky leaned over the table. "You know what next?" He stopped and glanced at Letty, who, fully dressed, emerged from the bathroom.

Dalton didn't want to know. It was enough that Port wasn't here, that the whole thing had turned out a failure.

"Next he gives Letty here a hard time. So I see red, you understand, Dalton? I see red. There's some buddies of mine at the dance and they seen what happened, so when Danny leaves they tip me off—"

Dalton closed his eyes, trying not to pay any attention. Half of the story that Dicky was telling sounded like lies, but that didn't matter. Port wasn't here; that mattered.

"—and I stop him right there in the alley. He was leaving by way of the alley, understand? So," Dicky shrugged, stared at the ash on his cigar, "what can I do? I beat him up."

Dicky let it hang there, hoping for a reaction from Dalton.

"Cut him down to size, you understand?"

"Yes," said Dalton.

"He's outa town now," Dicky said. "My buddies throwed him out—what was left of him." Dicky knocked the ashes off the end of his cigar.

All of it might have been lies, but what mattered was that Port wasn't here. Dalton remembered Port the way he had been and he didn't understand any of this. He did not have the strength to try and understand it, he just nodded and said, "Yes," again. He put his hands on the table and rubbed them together. His fingers were cold.

"I forgot to ask you," said Dicky. "You in? Or out?"

"Show me what you have," said Dalton.

It was getting dark, and after Letty put on her coat and left, Dicky got up and turned on the light which hung from the ceiling. There were paper cups on the table, stained brown inside with cold coffee. Dicky sat down again and pushed up his shirt sleeves. Dalton was rubbing the top of his head. He pulled at his open collar, and then stared at the papers again. There were loose sheets of scrap paper and a large, springy roll of blueprints.

"For a guy who don't want to, you're doing fine," Dicky said. "I'll grant you."

Dalton nodded but he had been doing that all along, without meaning. Just nodding. He reached for the bottle of milk at his elbow and took a small sip. The warm liquid revolted him but it dulled the pain.

"There isn't much more I can do," said Dalton. "To finish it off I need more information."

"You been saying that." Dicky stretched, making his shoulder joints crack.

Dalton put the papers in order, stacking most of them and crumpling some. Then he rolled up the blueprints.

"These are fine," he said, "unless they've changed the layout—added buildings or something."

"I told you the ground plans of that plant haven't changed. How often do I got to—"

"You go over it, and over it, and over it," said Dalton. He was tired too, but he was dogged and he was trying to work the way he used to. "So what you've got is the layout. Through the gate, cross the yard two hundred feet, pass the loading platform in front of shipping, and on past that. Next go to the right of the building—because you say there's a floodlight over the corner—and then take it from the parked trucks to the office building. Hit that through the front door, the shortest way. Hallway with time clock, up the stairs to the right to the second floor."

"You go straight and into the shop, Dalton, I told you there's another staircase going up to the—"

"First staircase from the hall," said Dalton. "You save

twenty-five feet and nobody sees you for the whole length of the shop."

"Jesus, Dalton, how often do I have to tell you there's more doors going your way! I'm trying to tell you—"

"Let me finish," said Dalton.

They were both tired and both irritated, each for his own reasons.

"A door is no problem compared to a watchman coming through the shop."

"I told you a hundred times they got just one making the rounds and he's got four buildings and a quarter mile of fencing to do and you keep—"

"Let me finish!"

Dicky looked startled. He kept still.

"You don't know his schedule," said Dalton. "You're only guessing. I don't plan with guesses." He sighed and let his voice drop again. "We'll get to that later. First, we finish with what we got." He thought for a moment to get his mind organized. "Second-floor hall door, corridor, south wall of typists' room. You don't know how many desks there are. You ought to know." Before Dicky could say anything Dalton went on. "Hit the safe ten minutes after passing the gate; do better, if possible." Dicky was rocking his chair back and forth, hardly listening. Dalton did not notice. "The safe—two hours at the outside. No lights. The way you knock it over has to be figured without lights."

"You said that, you said that—"

Dalton looked up. He showed no emotion this time. "I say it again and then over again. So you know where the holes are. So you do it right. The safe is in the typists' room with windows the length of the wall. There's a railroad siding a quarter of a mile from the plant with a freight standing there and you don't know when he's pulling out. Another thing you don't know." Dalton tapped his hand on the table. "Next. You got, let's say, three hours at the outside for the safe. You don't know what kind of safe, so we'll say three hours—"

"I told you! I told you it's a Milton and Dunn! Christ, how often do I got to tell you—"

"You told me nothing. Milton and Dunn made nine different safes and six different types of each in nineteen forty-one. I don't know what they make now. I haven't checked since then and you haven't given me the information. Next." Dalton traced a pencil over the blueprint. "Back the same way, till you hit the trucks. New route. Crating yard to the fence—" Dicky bit his lips and stared up at the ceiling. "You need a new route because you save five hundred yards to the getaway. Five hundred yards of doubling back with a load, and nervous. I wouldn't trust you back out on the road when it's over. Cut the fence; go through the north field to that path going back to the road. The car at the railroad crossing, by the junkyard with all the old cars, where the driver can see you come out of the field. He meets you going north and you're off."

Dalton stopped and Dicky got up, slapping his hands against his thighs.

"You done? Fine." He began to pace from one wall to the other. "I'm glad you're done repeating yourself because I like to get in a word edgewise. Okay, Dalton?" Dicky stopped pacing and gave Dalton a look, but the old man said nothing.

"Okay," Dicky said again. "Now here's how I got it figured, saving time. The watchman I don't worry about till we get there. I'll check him out myself. Same with the one at the gate. The train schedule I don't care about because I know for a fact no brakeman or anybody like that is gonna tell from a quarter of a mile away if there's an extra light in that plant or not. And if he does, he'll think it's the watchman coming through. So to hell with that. About the safe, you give me a guess. By the size and the make and the way the thing looks from the front, you can figure it's maybe this or that kind of lock. You take all the tools for what you think it might be and I get a man to carry the extra. That way we play it safe and no more horsing around with this planning. I been waiting long enough, Dalton. No more horsing around with that paperwork stuff." He looked at Dalton. "What now? You think up something else?"

"I didn't think it up. I just wasn't finished. You called three of the loopholes yourself. The guard, the train, the safe. Here's more. What's the alarm there, and where?"

"We don't break no windows, we don't have to worry."

"Does the safe have one? Did your man tell you?"

"No, he didn't tell me! How about you telling me?

You're so hot with safes from way back, how come you don't—"

Dalton held up his hand. Then he leaned over to ease his stomach. He took a deep breath and said, "Your man," he said. "Is he a sweeper who's casing for you, or is he a caser who hired out there as a sweeper?"

"What in hell is the difference! Listen, Dalton—"

"You listen to me," said Dalton. The grinding inside his stomach made him curt. "I don't make mistakes if I know about them ahead of time. There's too many here, before even starting. How come, Dicky? You used to learn a lot. How come all this slipshod planning?"

Dicky stopped short, wheeled and came around to Dalton's side of the table. He hunched his shoulders. His face got livid.

"I'm running this thing, and what I want from you is toeing the line!" he shouted. "I don't want you to keep watering down what I been planning and figuring and I don't want you to try running it like an old man's card game! I got this planned from way back just waiting for you to get out. I don't wait any more. I can't sit around any more waiting for something to happen, you hear?"

When Dicky stopped for breath Dalton said, "You're rushing it, Dicky."

Dicky didn't say anything for a second and then he grated, "How old were you when you pulled that railroad job, huh? That Southern Pacific job? The one that was all over the papers, and they never pinned it on you till the statute ran out?"

"I was twenty-one," said Dalton.

"And I'm in the middle of thirty, you old son of a bitch, so don't hold me up, you hear me?"

Dalton said nothing. Dicky didn't say any more. He went up to the table and started knocking the coffee containers over, one by one.

"Where in hell is that lamebrain?" he said and then he started cursing Letty.

Dalton picked up his bottle of milk. He swirled the liquid for a moment, hoping that he would not have to drink it. But the pain was big and blue now, a heavy pain that weakened him and made him want to lie down.

"So, like I was saying," Dicky started again, "you got this all clear?"

"Dicky," said the old man. "Please listen to me."

"You've done fine," said Dicky and went to the window where he leaned out looking for Letty.

"Dicky," said the old man. When Dicky pulled in his head and came back to the table Dalton said, "I agreed to come in with you. I wouldn't, except you got me over a barrel. So I'm in. When I'm in, Dicky, I do a thing right. The only thing I want out of this is to stay out of prison. You want more. You want a job that's—"

"What's coming, Dalton? What's on your mind?"

"Do it right, is all. Like the alarm. You don't know a thing about the alarm."

"Look," said Corday. He talked fast. His tone was insulting. "There's a box, see? That's the alarm, see? It rings to beat hell if you trip it, and the guard comes running, get the picture? There's a million ways, see? Like the one this guy told me about he seen in a picture. You squirt a fire extinguisher into the box and the thing won't ring, see? You didn't know about that, did you? You don't short the wires, you don't fool with the tripper—"

"May not work," Dalton said. "The alarm may ring at the nearest station. There's that kind."

Corday almost stopped breathing. He held himself in, to check the rage he could feel flushing his face.

Then both men heard the steps approaching the door and Dicky held on because he wanted Letty to see this. Her big, dumb eyes were going to look bigger than hell when she saw how Corday handled Dalton, the pro.

"It's my way," Dicky shouted suddenly, "or back to the rock. Clear enough, Dalton?" Dicky kept eying the door.

"Say so right now, Dalton! One way or the other!"

Dalton just sat at the table and the pain inside him made him look hunched and small. He wished Corday would stop.

"And from now on you hop! You got a million notions I don't have all the dope? Get it! I'll drive you down, Dalton, and you case that place all you want. I'll give you a day—two days, seeing how old and slow you are—and then we knock that place over!"

Dicky stopped, waiting for some reaction, but Dalton just sat.

"You got that straight, Dalton?" he heard Dicky shout. "And now jump!"

"Don't! And you either, Corday."

Port was there in the room. He slammed the door shut behind him.

## *Chapter 9*

Dicky stood crouched at the table, and he wished that there were more people watching this because the rage inside him made him feel as big as he wanted to be. Another step, Port, and another—

Port kept right on coming from the door to the table, and when Port swung the sudden, hard sound of his fist seemed to come out of nowhere.

Port stepped back to let Dicky fall and then took a deep breath. He waited for a while, but Dicky didn't move.

Dalton got out of his chair, not trusting himself to say anything yet, just staring at Port.

"You all right, Abe?" Port came closer.

Dalton nodded. His insides were churning, but he didn't feel it. It had all changed so quickly, Port coming back and Corday unconscious on the floor—

"What's this?" said Port and riffled through the notes and the stiff role of blueprints.

"When you didn't come," Dalton said, "when nothing happened—"

"Nothing happened?" said Port, and started to laugh. He stopped laughing quickly because of the pain that shot up the side of his chest.

"Sit down," said Dalton. "Maybe you shouldn't be on your feet. And a compress on that," he said, pointing at Port's left cheek.

A big scrape ran the length of Port's face from the temple down to the jaw, and when he moved Dalton noticed how Port kept one arm close to his ribs.

"How bad is it?" said Dalton. "Maybe you should . . ."

"I got away easy," said Port. He gave Dicky a brief look, then lit a cigarette and sat down. "The cops came to break it up. Or else he and his gang could have crippled me good." Port saw the stained paper cups on the table, but saw too that they were all empty. "That's why I'm late," he said. "I just got out of the cooler." He fingered the cups and waited for Dicky to wake up.

"Maybe you're too late, just the same," Dalton said. He waved at the notes and the rolled blueprints. "He's got me to start—"

Port looked at Dalton, and killed his cigarette in one of the cups.

"Just one thing, Abe." Port watched the old man and saw how sick he was. "You want out of this racket, or you want to stay in?"

Dalton started to raise his hands, then dropped them in a helpless gesture.

"It looks so— I don't know what to think, or to feel, Dan. It looks so far off—"

"I made it," said Port.

Dalton nodded and almost smiled.

"You're not sick. You don't have things hanging over you."

"Who doesn't?" said Port. "Is that what's stopping you?"

"There are things—like that job he's holding over my head—things you can't make up for."

"Maybe not. But you can stop doing them over."

"When I think," Dalton said. "When I think how I used to be—not sick—"

"That's why I'm helping you," Port told him. "If you want out."

"*If* I want out." Dalton paused. When he spoke again he was hardly audible. "I used to think that if I went back to prison, it'd kill me. I'd die." He closed his eyes. "That's not how it is, Dan. If I go back it'll be like living forever—and now that's the worst."

He bent over and didn't look up.

Port let go of the paper cup and went over to Dicky. He grabbed him under the arms, pulled him up, and tossed him into the chair.

"Pull out of it," he said and lifted Dicky's chin. Dicky moved his head. "Come on, you can make it," Port said and gave him a rough shake.

Dicky's face was silent and closed and Port started to frown. He caught on barely in time to get out of the way when Dicky kicked out with his foot. Dicky made it out of the chair and over to the wall with the dresser.

Port was boiling. Before Corday got the gun free of the top drawer Port was on top of him. Dicky leaned back over the dresser, gun held high, trying to reach Port with his knee. Port's left shot out aimed at the soft part where Dicky's ribs came together. Dicky doubled over and tried swinging the gun down like a club. Port slapped him sharply on the arm and Dicky, bending over, exposed the back of his neck.

He caught the rabbit punch there. It made his ears sing and his eyes burn and it shook up the insides of his head. He fell on his face, still conscious.

"On your feet," he heard Port say.

He balled himself up on the floor, tensed like a spring.

He heard Port curse and then felt himself yanked to his feet. Port's face was close to his. He hadn't known Port could look the way he did now.

"Corday, are you listening? Answer me!"

"Yes— I hear ya— Yes."

"You and me, Corday, we're through horsing around. You understand that?"

Dicky nodded. Then he nodded again because it made him feel as if his head were clearing.

"And pushing around, Corday. You're through pushing anyone around. You got that clear?"

Dicky's head was much better now. And Port didn't look as if he wanted to fight any more.

"And this heavy deal," said Port. He went to the table. "That's over." He picked up the notes and tore them in half. "And now I want to know how you were going to sing to the cops."

"Sing?" said Dicky. "I'm not gonna—"

Port came closer to Dicky and Dicky saw how Port was biting his lower lip, and how still Port's face looked.

"I mean I was gonna sing, like I kept telling Dalton, but there wasn't anything . . ."

Port waved impatiently. "What was it? Come on, Corday."

"I was gonna tell 'em . . ."

"No. You wouldn't have been this sure about Dalton. What was it you were going to show them?"

"Show them?"

"Corday," said Port. "I'm getting tired of asking."

But Dicky knew something about Port by now—that Port wouldn't start swinging again just for the hell of it, and that he was waiting to hear. A talker, try talking around him or even try— Dicky started to think in long, flicking jumps, so busy trying to think his way out of it that he started nervously at a sound at the door.

Letty came in. She had a large bag in her hand. She looked at Port standing, at Dalton crouched in his chair, and at Dicky, at the dresser, his hair all mussed.

She said, "Hello. I didn't know you'd still be talking. I thought . . ."

"Close the door," said Port.

She didn't know what was going on but she sensed the tension in the room.

"It's all right," said Port. "You can close the door." Then he stooped to the floor and picked up Dicky's gun. He pushed the cylinder open, and ejected the shells into his hand, and when he dropped them into his pocket he began to whistle softly. He tossed the gun onto the bed.

"Did you bring some coffee?" he asked the girl.

Letty closed the door and went to the table. She put her packages down and opened the carton of coffee. White steam lifted off the black liquid. "There're some cups on the dresser," she said.

"Thank you."

Port held his hand out toward Dicky, who took a cup off the dresser and gave it to Port.

"You didn't finish your milk," said Letty. She looked at Dalton. "I brought you more."

Dalton said, "Thank you," but he sounded as if he were hardly there. When Letty pushed the small carton across to him he didn't touch it.

She made more sounds with the paper bag, pulled out a hamburger, and then another one. The room was quiet. Everyone just stood around. Then Port went into the bathroom to run some cold water into his coffee. They all listened to the sound of the water running and looked at the bathroom door. When Port came back into the room no one had moved.

It would depend on Port, Dicky thought. He could figure this thing once Port made his move. But for the moment Port just stood by the wall, holding his cup in both hands. Now and then he took a sip. He watched Dalton, who sat in his chair looking as if he had been beaten.

"There's two ways we can do this," Port said without transition. "Are you listening, Abe?"

Dalton looked up and nodded.

"We can do it straight, or we can really cross him up."

Dicky frowned, not understanding it.

"I don't care which way we do it," said Port. "Seeing it's Dicky at the receiving end."

"What do you mean?" Dalton leaned his arms on the table, trying to ignore the sharp stings inside him.

"We can do it straight and ask Corday here to hand over the evidence, whatever he's got."

Corday was starting to sweat. They were talking about him as if he were something you bought in a store.

"Or, if he thinks he's too smart for a straight deal, we can play it crooked." Port sipped some coffee, and then went on. "He can go ahead with his heist, but somewhere along the line he'll get crossed up. But good."

"Wait a minute." Corday came away from the dresser, but standing alone in the middle of the room suddenly made him self-conscious. He went back to the dresser and started to talk very fast. "Wait. You don't know what you're doing. Hell, you can't pull that on me! Or Dalton! You can't pull this on Dalton! Hell—" Dicky was loud and excited. "You'd do a thing like a doublecross? How crooked can you get?"

Port waited to see if Dicky had finished and then he said, "Not that crooked. Don't forget, I'm telling you ahead of time."

"I don't want it that way, Dan," Dalton said quietly. "If I say I'm going to do it, I'll do it. I told Dicky I wasn't going through with it, but if I ever say yes I'll do it."

"That's right," said Corday. "He's straight, anyway. He don't . . ."

"So we'll do it the other way," Port said. "Show me what you think will make Dalton work with you."

"Hell," Dicky started again, "I been telling you . . ."

"I'm through stalling!" Port was suddenly loud. He put down his cup and came a step closer.

Letty was watching. Arguing with Port might hold off

things a while longer, but Letty was there, watching.

Dicky went to the closet and reached into the lining of one of his suits. When he felt what he wanted he hesitated for a moment. A lot rode on this thing—was he going to give it away?

"It's in there," said Letty. "Can't you find it, Dicky?"

Corday didn't say anything, but right then he hated her guts. He hated her guts for being there, for watching, for butting in and for being Letty.

"You're taking too long," Port said behind him.

Dicky wiped the sweat from his face and came back into the room. He had some folded papers in his hand, held together with a rubber band.

"Here." He tossed the small bundle on top of the table. "The works. It's worth . . ."

"Just shut up," said Port and picked up the papers.

"Dead to rights," Dicky said, chattering. "I got him dead to rights! This can . . ."

"You recognize this?" Port showed the papers to Dalton.

". . . this can mean a mint, don't you get it? This can mean Dalton doing one job after another, big ones—" Nobody was listening to him but Dicky went on talking excitedly. "All right, so he's old maybe. Maybe he ain't so good any more at pulling a heist, but so what. I can see him laying it out—he doesn't have to go on the job, just lay it out. Sit in his chair and plan the job."

"Stop dreaming," said Port. Then, to Dalton, "What's he got on you here?"

Dalton went through the papers. One had a drawing on it, a ground plan of a building, studded with arrows and notes. Another sheet had a time schedule on it, a detailed schedule with minute-by-minute instructions—a well-planned blueprint for cracking a safe.

Dalton still looked sick, but excited now. His hands shook when he pushed the papers across the table.

"The Exchange Bank—that small town in Idaho—Bexley." He got up and stared at Dicky, furious now. "I never pulled that heist! I wasn't in it!"

There was a small silence. Dicky and Dalton stared at each other and then Dicky yelled, "That bank was knocked over in forty-one by this plan! And the plans here. They're in your handwriting, right?"

Dalton sat down again. The fury had gone out of his face but he was still excited. He sat down, reached for the bottle of milk and took a long swallow. Some of the milk ran down the side of his mouth.

"Abe," said Port. "Explain this."

Dalton put down the bottle and swallowed hard.

"I wasn't in on that job. It's my handwriting, yes, but I wrote that out later, much later, for Dicky. I knew about the job and how they were doing it and I wrote it all out for him, to show him how it was done. That's all!" he shouted. "That's all it is! I was never in on that job! I mean it—believe me!"

For a moment Port thought that this might end it. There was nothing here that could force Dalton back into jail—but the thought lasted only a moment. He did not think it was over. He looked out the window. He wished he were not here.

Then Dicky started to laugh. "He wasn't in on the job? So what! It looks like he was, and if not—so what!"

Port watched Dalton get out of his chair and go to the window. He was walking badly. He went to the window and stretched his neck as if fighting for air. Dicky saw it too, and laughed louder.

"Abe," said Port and went after the old man. He put his hand on Dalton's back. "Just hold out, Abe. We'll make it," he said softly. Then he turned back to the room.

"Corday," he said, "you got a point. And here's mine."

He didn't get any further. Dicky began to shout.

"You got plans, maybe, to take that evidence there on the table and tear it up like you did with the notes? Go ahead, Port, take it. And the first move you make, I yell cop. This hotel's got a regular pipeline to the next precinct. Wanna bet? Grab that evidence, and I yell cop. They'll find the stuff here unless you eat it. And if you do I can still make it hot." He stopped, and then his laugh came battering out again. "They'll find Dalton here. Dalton—you know—he's still on parole. He's on parole and associating with criminal elements. Me, a crook that served time, and you a crook that got away. They'll go hard on Dalton, understand?"

Port had tried waiting it out expressionlessly, but the more Dicky talked the closer Port got to losing his temper. It must have showed in his face because Dicky suddenly changed the tone of his voice. Now he was wheedling.

"Port, listen to me. I'll give you a chance. I shoulda caught on to you sooner, but better late than never. Listen!" Dicky leaned over the table. "I'll cut you in," he said hoarsely. "We can share the old man!"

"You make me sick," Port said.

All it meant to Corday was no, that he had missed the angle, that he didn't know the price.

"What?" he said. "What more? You want half? You want more than half? You wanna pick your own crew? Port, just don't foul up this job! Anything within reason."

"Dicky, please, I don't think you know—"

They had both forgotten about the girl. They looked at Letty where she sat on the bed and the silence made her lose her nerve.

Corday suddenly hated her guts. Hating Letty and fearing Port he went to the bottom and tried his last.

"You save me this setup, Port, and I'll trade you big. Here, take her! You want her? She's a lamebrain, but what the hell. Look what I'm trading you! She's . . ."

There was a dull sound from over near the window and Dalton sagged into a heap. He made only a small clatter.

"My God!" Letty was off the bed and standing over Dalton. "He's sick!"

Port knelt on the floor and turned the old man on his back. When the door slammed he looked up and there was only Letty in the room. Port did not have to look at the table to know that the plans in Dalton's writing were no longer there.

Port got up. There was no phone in the room and he went toward the door. He had to pass Letty. Before he passed her he stopped. He stood very close to her.

"He loves you?" he said, and then he went out.

## *Chapter 10*

Port called the fire department because their ambulance service was the fastest. They came without a doctor so Port did not find out why Dalton had fainted. When the ambulance left Port stayed behind at the hotel.

Dicky's car was not on the street and the hotel desk clerk knew nothing. Port went to the stairs, but he did not go up because Letty came down, dressed for the street. She came into the lobby, saw Port, but said nothing to him. She went to the desk and gave the clerk her key. Port watched her do it and close her purse afterwards. When she looked up she looked out to the street, past Port's shoulder.

Her face seemed shut and the look of just waking up was gone.

She walked to the door, and then she stopped and waited for Port.

"Are you looking for Dicky?" she asked him.

"Can you help?"

She walked out onto the street and pointed left so that Port would know which way they were going. He did not try to talk to her. After ten minutes Letty stopped at a corner and nodded.

"You see where it says Sport Parlor?"

Port saw the gold letters on the plate window.

"I have to go in there," she said. "That's his place—I mean where his friends are, and maybe they know."

"I'll go in," said Port. "I don't think women are welcome there."

"You think you are?" she said. "There's a diner, down this way. I'll meet you there."

She left Port and went towards the Sport Parlor.

They saw her coming when she crossed the street, and they all straightened up from the pool table to watch her. They knew her because she was Dicky's and because they all had grown up together in the same streets. They saw her stop for a passing car and then come toward the pool hall again. They saw her legs where the skirt ended and the way she set her feet. They saw the way her hips moved when she took a step. They watched the button that held her coat closed in the middle over her breasts.

"Here's your chance, Mac," one of them said, and they all looked at Mac to see how he would react.

"I ain't like you guys. I don't have to hang outa the window and imagine."

"Imagine, my foot! Lookit her. That's all solid, man. I mean solid."

They all looked out the pool-hall window and imagined what Letty was like.

And then, "Jesus—she's coming in!"

When Letty came into the pool-hall they all stood by the table and looked at her. She stopped in the aisle between the cigar counter and the big tables. She wished they would not look at her with waiting stares.

"Have you seen Dicky?" she said. "I'm looking for Dicky."

"Dicky?" said Mac. Then he looked at his buddies. "She needs Dicky," he said.

They all laughed, loudly and rawly.

Letty stood in the aisle and held her purse in both hands. She held it low, as if she were naked.

"Tell you what, though," said Mac. He hitched his rear onto the edge of the table and started swinging one leg. Then he grinned so everybody would know that now the next one came, and they should get ready.

"I'll tell you what, Letty. I'll play you some pool." He laughed loudly and they all joined in.

Letty waited for them to finish. She would have liked to leave but she stayed where she was and waited. The men at the table saw her take a deep breath. They saw that she did not mean to leave.

"You know where he is," she said. "I've got to find him."

"Oh," said Mac. "It's that way."

But this time nobody laughed. Letty had changed their mood for them.

Mac turned back to the table and picked up a cue stick. He started making passes at the low-number ball but didn't hit.

"A Coke, Letty?" he said, without turning around.

Letty had to walk to the table because all of them had followed Mac's lead. They had all turned away to watch the game.

"I don't want to bother you," Letty said, "I just want to ask . . ."

She broke off short because Mac moved his cue back and the butt of the stick nudged Letty in the soft of her stomach.

"Gee, I'm sorry," said Mac. "Where'd I tap you, here?" and he gave her a pat.

When Letty tried stepping out of his way she got caught from behind.

"Here," said the one who was holding her. "Mac didn't mean nothing, kid. Here, stand over by me." His hands held her arms from behind.

"Duff, she don't want you either," said Mac. "Come here, Duff, let her go."

But Duff didn't. He got next to Letty and put one arm around her. He kept his face close to the girl's and said something into her ear.

"All *I* asked her was to play pool," said Mac and they all stood back laughing and watching how Duff held onto the girl.

"Lemme go " said Letty. "Lemme go." The more she struggled the more they laughed and kept watching. She dropped her purse, her coat opened, and someone pulled it off her back. The laughing got much more quiet and a slow tension grew over the group. It wasn't just Duff now, holding her. They had all come close.

She could scream, she could weep, she thought she might faint, but Letty knew none of this would help her. They were all silent now. She heard only her own breathing. She caught a glimpse of the man at the counter, a fat man who had been asleep. He was awake now and watching. He had come to the end of the counter and stood there holding his lip in his teeth.

They were not really pawing her, they were pushing her one way. They had turned her so that she could see one of them holding a door open, waiting.

Letty moved by instinct. She didn't plan it or think it out.

"Jesus, you can let go. Don't you know that?"

They did let go. They stood there startled by her tone, by the lassitude in the movement she made when she pushed the hair out of her face. She put her hands on her hips. She took a deep breath and let it go. She ran her tongue over her teeth and said, "How many of you guys are there?"

They looked at each other but nobody spoke. One of them tried to laugh but it came out more like a cough.

"I'm asking," said Letty. "Whatsamatter, you never done business before? The rate goes by the number."

The man in the back closed the door.

"Get off my coat," said Letty and the man who had stepped on the hem of her coat moved away quickly.

"Give it to her," said Mac. "Ain't you got no manners?"

They gave her the coat and the purse, and they started to drift back to the table.

"Hell," said Mac, "how come you getting so serious, Letty? We was kidding around, is all, just trying to kid you."

Letty said, "Yeah?"

"Sure. Just fooling, you know?"

"I'm not," she said.

"Sure, Letty. And besides, we're Dicky's friends. Don't you know that? You ought to know that."

She tossed her coat over her shoulders, and when she followed them to the table, the coat flounced back and forth behind her.

"Sure," she said. "While he's around, maybe."

Duff started to line up a shot, then sank a ball. Mac was chalking.

"You got us wrong, Letty. What the hell, he's not gone for good. He'll be back, Dicky will."

"When?"

"When? I don't know. Duff, you know when?"

Duff straightened up and said, "Huh?" He looked very much interrupted.

"When's Dicky coming back? You got mud in your ears? Letty here wants to know when . . ."

"Oh, sure. He said maybe a week. Takes a day each way and he figures on a few days there."

"There? Where?" said Letty. "I asked you a dozen times."

"Oh, Newton. This burg Newton. You know."

"Yeah," said Letty. "The job." She looked down when she said it and opened her purse so that her face wouldn't show. She did not know how she might look. It was getting to be too much for her. Dicky was going to do it himself, rushing it for some reason, changing everything he had planned—

"Didn't he tell you?" said Duff.

"Sure, but I must have heard wrong. I thought he said next week. I thought—"

She was glad when she was interrupted. She did not know what to say next, and she was afraid that she could not carry it off for much longer. Anxiety touched her.

"He didn't know it himself," said Mac, "the way he came in here, all steamed. What happened? He wouldn't say."

"He thinks somebody is trying to butt in. That's why, I guess."

"Sure. He come in here asking for Loony. He needs Loony right away, so when we tell him that Loony's at work he hightails right outa here and to the shop."

"The shop?"

"Where Loony's working. That's why he's called Loony. He works in a shop." Mac laughed.

They all laughed, glad for the change.

"Maybe they know at the shop—" Letty started, but saw that she had made a mistake.

"You crazy or something? That's a legitimate job Loony's got there. They don't know from anything else. Christ—women!" said Mac and turned to the table.

"Christ, yes," somebody else said. "You want Loony to lose his job?"

"Maybe he'll lose it anyway," said Duff between shots. "The way he keeps taking off."

"Him? He's skilled. They don't fire the skilled ones."

They were through with Letty. They had a topic to haggle over, and they were absorbed in it. They turned it back and forth and held on to it, because it was better than boredom.

"He's always got a job. Hell, he can walk into any town—"

"That's what he said. He come in here for his cigars before taking off with Dicky, don't you remember? He come in here—"

"I was kidding him about getting fired. That's right—"

". . . and he says he's taking a job in this burg. What was the name of this burg—"

Letty was at the door, no longer listening. She went out into the street. She went only as far as the end of the building, where she could not be seen from the pool-hall. Port was waiting and she would tell him all she could remember. But first she had to stop. She leaned against the brick wall and breathed deeply. She did this until she felt sure that the trembling would not start again.

## *Chapter 11*

PORT sat in the diner and tried looking the length of the street, but the window faced the wrong way. There were three cigarettes in his ashtray, the charred ends pushed flat. He moved his cup by the handle, moving it back and forth until some coffee spilled. Then he dragged his saucer over the puddle so that the stain would not show.

He did not see Letty until the draft from the door made him turn. She came to the booth, sat opposite Port, and said, "He left town. He . . ."

They had to wait while the waitress asked for the new order and until she got back with two cups of coffee. Letty didn't touch hers and Port pushed his own out of the way.

"You have any trouble?" Port asked her.

Letty looked at her handbag. "He left town," she said again. "He went to that Newton place." The concern showed in her face. "I think—"

"For how long? Do you know?"

"They said maybe a week. Do you think he's trying to do it alone?"

Port didn't know. He picked up his cup, but found the coffee too hot. He put the cup down again. "He's off the old man, anyway. He's not pushing him any more."

"Yes," she said. "That's good." She snapped her bag open and closed it again. "But do you think he should—do you think he's doing it on his own?"

Port looked up and gave her a brief smile.

"You worried about him?"

She said, "A little. He's no good at it—"

"If he gets caught maybe that'll mean something to him."

"He's been in before. The same thing. The second time they won't go easy."

"How come you're worried about him?"

"I don't like to see anyone go to prison."

Port looked out of the window and nodded at nothing. Then he turned back. "I don't know any of the details about this Newton job. I don't know if one man can do it alone."

"He didn't go by himself. He took Loony along."

"Loony?"

"He's somebody works in the shop down the next street. Dicky took him."

"They work together before?"

"I don't know what Loony does. He works in that shop."

Port frowned at the table. "Maybe he will try it alone. You'll just have to sweat it out."

He got out of the booth, put some change under his cup, and reached for Letty's arm.

"Try not to worry about it," he said. "Will you, Letty?"

"Sure," she said. "I'll try."

Port held the door for her and they went out into the street. "I'll take you home now," he said. "And thanks very much for your help." He paused. "Looks like rain." He took her arm to make her walk faster.

They turned the corner and Port saw the shop down the street. It said, *South Side Machine Co.,* and underneath, Toolmakers and Diemakers.

"That's where Loony works?" Port nodded at the small shop.

"Yes. He's something skilled, they said,"

They walked by the shop.

"Toolmakers and diemakers," said Port. "The next best thing to being a locksmith—for Dicky's purposes."

It started to rain in slow drops and they walked bent over.

"You going after him?" Letty asked.

"No. There's no point."

The rain got heavier and they put their heads down, seeing only their feet.

"Will you let me know when Dicky gets back?" Port asked.

She didn't answer right away. She wiped rain off her nose and bit her lip.

"I don't know," she said. "I—I don't know yet." She looked at Port seriously. "You know what I mean?"

"Sure," said Port, and he nodded.

"Where do you live?" she asked.

"I'm leaving town," said Port. "I'll call you when I get back."

They turned into the door of the hotel and stood on the mat for a moment, shaking the rain off their clothes. Port felt the dampness through the back of his suit and he saw where Letty's coat had soaked through. She shook off the coat and moved her shoulders to keep the wet dress from clinging.

"You want to come up?" she said. "To dry off?"

"No," said Port, "Thanks. I'll come up just to get those notes out of the way. We left Dalton's notes on the table."

"I threw them into the wastebasket," she said. "Before the men from the ambulance came."

"I'll get them," said Port. They went to the desk to get Letty's key, and then they went upstairs.

The desk clerk made no comment and nobody saw them go up because the lobby was empty. There was just a man in the doorway who stood there shaking the rain out of his hair. He looked at them very briefly and then went out into the street again.

Letty closed the door to her room while Port went to the wastebasket. She watched him pull the torn papers out, stuff them into his pocket and then straighten up. She waited until he looked at her.

"And I want to thank you," she said, "for not pushing me."

"About what?"

"About Dicky. About helping you go after Dicky."

"I'm not really after him," Port said. "As long as he doesn't push the old man."

She went to the bed and sat down and pushed her shoes off with her feet. It struck Port as a tired gesture.

"Maybe Dicky will learn that, when he comes back," she said. She got off the bed and walked toward the bathroom. She had started unbuttoning the top of her dress.

"You're wet too," she said. "Can I make you some coffee? I got this hotplate over there"—and she nodded at it from the bathroom door.

Port thought she looked very tired. He thought it might have something to do with the way she felt about Dicky.

"No, thanks," he said. "I've got to go." He waved at

her from the door and walked rapidly from the room.

When Port walked through the lobby the desk clerk looked up without interest, then looked back at the book he was holding. One page had print on it and the facing page a palmist's chart of a hand. The clerk was absorbed in it. Then a man stepped to the desk and the clerk looked up. He said, "Hi, Mac. Wet out?"

"Anyone else with her?"

"Who?"

"Dicky's dame."

"No," said the clerk.

"No visitors for an hour," said Mac, and went up the stairs. The clerk looked back at the chart again.

When Letty heard the door open she stopped shaking her dress out and closed her bathrobe in front.

"That's all right," said Mac. He leaned against the bathroom door and folded his arms.

"Please," said Letty. "Please go."

"That was fast," said Mac. He acted as if she hadn't said anything. "You and him, I mean. That bastard we beat up at the dance hall."

"He just walked me home," Letty said, not knowing what else to say. She did not think it would make much difference what she might say now.

"He in on this deal?"

"What? I don't know what—"

"He's butting in on Dicky, right? Dicky said so."

"He's leaving town. He just told me, Mac. Really, he's not even interested—"

"Leaving town? Coming back when?"

"I don't know. But he'll call me. When he comes back he'll call me up, and if you really want to know—"

"He gone to Newton?"

"Oh no. I told you, he's not . . ."

"But he's leaving, huh? A few days, a week?"

"More like a week. It sounded like a week. And when he left he . . ."

"That's okay," said Mac, "you done fine." He pushed away from the door and took Letty's arm.

It opened her bathrobe on top and she let it be. There was no point in trying to close it again.

Mac stayed for an hour. Then he left, got in his car, and drove out of town towards Newton.

## *Chapter 12*

"WE ARE very glad you showed up," said the old woman at the reception desk. "He hasn't been able to answer questions."

"All right," said Port. "Then can I see him?"

"We'll call the floor," said the old woman. "After you fill out this form."

The clinic receiving desk was very busy and Port had to wait while the woman attended to something else. Then she took him into the office behind the desk while she searched for the form with the name Abraham Dalton at the top.

"What would you like to know?" Port tried to prompt her.

"The fire department brought him," she said. "There was a fire?"

"There was no fire. There was an emergency and . . ."

"Why didn't you call our service? Our drivers have their instructions about forms for Receiving. We always . . ."

"It was an emergency," Port said again.

"Nevertheless." She got up to get a bottle of ink so that she could fill her fountain pen.

For the next twenty minutes Port gave her Dalton's name again, because she wanted to hear it, Dalton's age, Dalton's address, and the facts that he was retired and had no known relatives.

"You want me to call the floor now?" the woman finally asked.

"Yes, please." Port sat watching her while she phoned Dalton's floor and explained that there was a visitor to see him.

"The nurse wants to know what the purpose of your visit is. Actually, the patient should not be seen for the next twelve hours. Actually . . ."

"I'm from the parole board," said Port. "Official business."

"Parole board? Dear—dear me—you mean Mr. Dalton is a criminal?"

"Was."

"Why didn't you say so? Why didn't you see to it that this fact was entered when I filled out the form?"

"I did." Port nodded at the form on the desk. "Former residence: Joliet. What did you think Joliet was?"

"Why—there's a town. I have a cousin in Joliet who's lived there for ten years."

"So did Mr. Dalton. May I go up now?"

There was some more hurried conversation on the phone and then Port got his pass. He took the elevator up to the second floor, gave his pass to a nurse who looked at it casually, and was led to a ward.

There were ten clean, white beds, with curtains between them, and progress reports hanging at their feet.

"Number Five," said the nurse, pointing, and left Port at the door. There was another nurse inside the ward. She sat at a small table where the row began and Port had to tell her whom he wanted to see.

"Number Five," she said, and smiled.

It was the first smile Port had seen in the place. He stopped at her table and said, "I'm the one who committed the patient. I wonder . . ."

"Only a physician can commit a patient. Are you his physician?" She smiled again. Port shook his head and smiled back.

"I called the ambulance was what I meant. Mr. Dalton had fainted. Could you tell me what happened?"

She reached for her records.

"Are you a relative?"

"He doesn't have any. About this fainting, I know he has a bad stomach—what's left of it."

She looked at the record. "He had a hemorrhage. Active ulcer. You knew that, I suppose."

"I don't know a thing. How bad is it?"

She looked again, moving her lips, and then put the record away.

"We don't know yet. His red count dropped badly in the beginning but it's leveled off now. If the bleeding doesn't start again he may improve slowly."

"May?" he said, and the nurse saw him frown.

"I can't tell you any more," she said. "Number Five. And just very briefly, all right?"

She smiled again and Port nodded. He walked down the row to the the fifth bed. He did not recognize Dalton.

A tube that hung from a red bottle was taped to his arm and a tube that hung from a white bottle was taped to his nose. His nose looked very large. His face looked sunken and only his nose seemed to be the same.

"Abe?"

Dalton was awake. He rolled his eyes and when he saw Port he smiled with just his mouth.

"Dan," he said. "How are you?" He sounded very strange to Port. "Come around this way."

Port moved around the bed so that Dalton would not have to roll his eyes so far and Port would be able to hear him better. He sat on a chair next to the bed and leaned close.

"You're getting better," he said. "I just asked the nurse. The one that smiles."

"That's nice," said Dalton and closed his eyes.

"And I'm not to stay long, Abe. Can I ask you something right away, so it won't take long?"

Dalton opened his eyes, waiting.

"That Bexley job, the one Dicky is holding over you—where were you when that was pulled?"

Dalton was about to make a gesture but the needle in his arm stopped him. He bit his lip and lay still for a moment. Then he said, "That was in forty-one."

"I know, Abe. A long time ago. But you must have been some place, and wherever you were, maybe somebody remembers. You see how that would clear you, Abe?"

Dalton did not answer.

"Maybe Florida—New York—prison, maybe—or some small town where you holed up. Chicago?"

"I know where I was." Port waited, and then Dalton said, "There's no point, Dan. Just forget it. Let it go. I'm safer now than I ever was."

Port looked away for a moment because he did not want Dalton to see that he was shocked. He did not know whether Dalton was right and would not live long enough to fear anything else.

"Abe, listen to me."

"I'm listening."

"You can't live the way things have been for you. It keeps you sick, don't you know that? You can live, though, the way you had planned it. You can go home, have a room of your own, an easy job in the small town where you came from—" Port watched the old man, and saw how Dalton was trying to keep his face expressionless. "You let me help you, Abe, and pin down a witness, and you can go home. You know that, don't you?"

"I know."

"Well?"

"I—I don't want to, Dan. I don't think I can."

"Will you tell me why? Will you at least tell me why?"

Dalton looked up at the ceiling and said, "I was with a woman. She was a young girl then and now she's a woman. She has a husband and two or three children. You can't do it."

"To save your life, Abe?"

"She may not remember."

"Why not?"

"We lived together. For a while. I don't think she loved me or anything."

"Abe. Listen to me. Just to help a man who's down like you are, for that you don't have to love, the way you meant. She has to be a human being. She just has to have some feeling . . ."

"She had that," said Dalton. "But she's got a life now, different. Why should she spoil—"

"She won't. And you won't. I'll keep in mind how you feel, Abe. I won't give her any trouble. I'll just ask her, in a friendly way, to give a little help. That's all. She won't ever get involved the way this can be handled. Come on, Abe. Who? Where?"

"I don't know—"

"Where? Tell me. Look, maybe she'll be glad to hear from you. I can give her your regards, at least that—"

It was lame, but Port didn't know what else he could do.

And then Dalton said, "She might. She was nice. Eve Tomlin was her name. Eve Simmon now."

"Where, Abe?"

"Same town, Otter Bend. In Minnesota."

Port got up and touched Dalton's shoulder.

"See you, Abe. In a few days."

Dalton nodded as Port stepped away from the bed. "If she remembers," he said, "give her my best."

## Chapter 13

THE TRAIN made the best connection to Otter Bend, and it took almost two days. There was a change on the second day, and at five in the morning Port stood for half an hour on a small, windy platform. He noticed how much colder it was here. Across the tracks was a young stand of pines, the tops whipping and twisting in the wind that came from the north. The tips of the trees had a silvery sheen, like hoarfrost.

There was a waiting room in the station, but Port stayed outside. The waiting room was not warm and had the feeling of a basement.

Two days both ways made four, leaving Dicky three days at the outside for his job. Port did not think he would need three days. If it took him three days it wouldn't be any good. He walked the length of the platform and felt the wind tugging at him. When the train came he sat by the window and watched how the landscape got bigger with wind-bare stretches and old woods getting deeper. Then he closed his eyes and slept most of the day.

The wind had stopped and Otter Bend looked warm in the late sun. The town did not look very large. Port could see almost all of it from the station platform. There was a long sheep shed along one side of the station and a diner opposite that. The town was behind the diner. The main street was short and very wide. Port could see the bank, the chain store, and the three car-dealer showrooms. The side streets had trees that were taller than most of the houses because there wasn't a building in town higher than two floors.

Port wondered whether he was looking at Eve Simmon's house. He picked up his bag, and went into the diner and sat down at the counter. There was a rancher at one end reading a two-page paper. A young boy with crowded teeth leaned his hands on the counter and asked Port what he would have.

"A cup of coffee," said Port. "Black."

The counterman drew the coffee and when he set the cup down it was half filled with milk. Port didn't say anything. He started drinking the coffee right away because it was cold enough.

"That all you want?" said the counterman.

Port put his cup down and pushed it over.

"Another cup, please. Black this time."

The counterman went to the urn and when he had drawn the coffee he turned and said, "That was black?"

"Black," said Port.

It was black and Port leaned over the cup to blow on the coffee.

"Anything else?" the counterman said.

"No, thanks."

The counterman took out a toothpick and started working inside his mouth. "My name's Curtis," he said. "What's yours?"

The boy was abrupt, Port thought, but all right otherwise, just eager for conversation.

"My name's Dan. How are you, Curtis?"

"Fine. You just off that train?"

"Yes. Just stopping over."

"Friends? Relatives? Business? You don't mind my asking do you? Uh, what was your name again?"

"Dan."

"That's right. Dan. You don't mind my asking, do you, Dan?"

"No, go ahead. As a matter of fact I'm going to ask you a few things myself. You don't mind, do you, Curtis?"

"No. that's fine, Dan. That's fine with me." He leaned his elbows on the counter and lowered his voice. "I can always do with some intelligent conversation, if you know what I mean." Curtis looked sideways at the rancher who was still reading his paper. "I get to talk with everybody comes in here, you understand, but I mean intelligent conversation. These guys here—" He jerked his head at the rancher and made a face.

"He can hear you," said Port.

"Naw. He's deaf. And what if he could? He wouldn't

know what I'm talking about. None of 'em do." Curtis sighed.

"I know what you mean," said Port and nodded seriously.

"I was born and reared here myself," Curtis said, "but I been away. I seen something, you know what I mean, and coming back after that—you know what I mean."

"Been around, huh?"

"Sure. I was in the Army."

"Ah," said Port. Then he picked up his coffee and tried it. It was lukewarm and he drank some of it.

"So where you from, Dan?"

"Chicago."

"Ah. That's a town."

"It certainly is, Curtis."

"I'll say." Curtis threw his toothpick away. "What's your business, Dan?"

"I'm in development. We represent production concerns interested in extending potential."

"Man. That's big business."

"Oh, yes."

"I'll say. And you're doing some of that up here, in this town?"

"Yes. Part of my job is incepting demand levels. I mean reconnoiter for incepting and at the same time recreate into repeater-consumption the senescent levels. That's how I get to see old customers too."

"That's a job!"

"I'll say. I don't repair them, you understand, but then they hardly ever need any repairing."

"Boy."

"Our line is for any part of the house, so you can imagine that our replacement department can't also be contained in the function of my division."

"No. Sure. I see that. Uh, are they expensive?"

"Not for the service. Anywhere from one-five to three-eighty-nine."

"Is that so? And they all work the same?"

"Sure. Just more chrome on the expensive ones. You know how it is."

"Hell, yes!"

"So I've got an introductory list of some customers here,

and maybe I'll look some of them up. Just good will, you understand."

"Sure. How about new ones? You after new ones?"

"No. Not really. We don't need them, you see."

"Oh."

"You know everyone in town, don't you, Curtis?"

"I sure do. Anyone you want to know about?"

"Brown," said Port, "and there's—"

"Jimmy or Melvin?"

"Both. And Simmon—"

"Yeah. Him too."

"Where?"

"The store. That's on the left, the main street, where it says Simmon Hardware. He's there till eight or nine, mostly."

"Fine. And where do I catch him at home?"

"Elm Road. There's no elms there but they call it that. The big frame house with the lantern out front."

"And the Browns?" Port asked, to round out the conversation. After that he said Mrs. Eve Simmon was one of their best customers, to make sure the Simmon on Elm Street was the one he really wanted. Then he paid for his coffee and got up to leave. He had his bag in his hand when Curtis said, "Psst!"

Port turned back. He remembered for no special reason that nobody had said "Psst" to him since he had been a boy.

"I know how it is with you big concerns," Curtis said, "about forms and so forth." He hesitated when he saw Port frowning. "And, of course, you got this policy you been telling me of, about no new customers."

"Yes," said Port. "It would create competition. The complex kind. Creeping socialism, you know—"

"Yeah, I know all that, but just between you and me, Dan, one of those dollar-five kind—how about it, Dan, could you—"

"Out of the question." Port went to the door.

"Look I got the money right here, Dan." Curtis was holding a dollar and a nickel in his hand.

"Out of the question," said Port and opened the door. "It would cost eight bucks in bookkeeping alone."

"Hey, Dan—"

"I'll send you a catalog. That way it's cheaper." He got through the door before Curtis could say anything more.

Elm Street was not very far. Port walked past the Simmon hardware store and Elm Street branched off that. There was a hotel at the corner, a frail-posted building with a narrow porch running along Main Street and around into Elm. Port went inside. There was no train out of Otter Bend that night so he would have to sleep over. He signed the register and left without having looked at the room. He carried his bag. He would call at the Simmons' home looking like a salesman.

It would help if the husband were not there. Port went back to the hardware store and looked through the window. There was a confusion of tools and implements on display but Port saw no one so he went inside. When he saw the boy at the counter Port walked toward him, keeping his back partially turned. He walked as far as the boy that way and looked at the middle aisle.

"You know," he said, "you used to have—" Then he turned to the counter and laughed. "I thought I was talking to Simmon. I guess he's . . ."

"He's out back. Selling a tiller," said the boy.

"Good old Simmon, always selling something," said Port. "I thought maybe he'd be up home. Supper time." Port nodded at the clock on the wall. It was six.

"He's been and back," said the boy.

"Fine. I'll be in before closing."

"He's closing at nine," said the boy.

"Fine," said Port and went out.

With luck it would take until seven, maybe eight. Then back to the hotel, a shower if there was one, and, if it wasn't too late, a call to Dalton. A message for Dalton in bed with the tubes: *All set. Get well. Dan.* Or something like that.

It was a very large, very neat frame house, with a well-kept lawn, white curtains and milk-glass figurines in the windows. On the front porch was a bicycle, a tricycle and a foot-pedal car.

Eve Simmon had at least three children, and she baked her own bread. Port saw the loaves on the sill of a side window and he smelled the fresh smell of them.

He went to the front door and rang the bell. He could

not see through the cut glass in the door but he heard steps almost immediately. When the door opened he said, "Mrs. Simmon?"

He barely caught a glimpse of the woman. He saw her shake her head. "I'm sorry, my husband isn't home," she said and the door closed again.

"I've just come from the store," he called through the door. "Mrs. Simmon. Your husband is at the store. I've just come from there!" He gave his voice a tone of alarm.

The woman opened the door again, all the way this time. She was frowning.

"Yes?" she said. "Is anything—"

"No," said Port. "May I come in?" He walked through the door.

He watched her close it. She closed it quickly, worried now.

Two children came into the hall, a girl of about four and a boy of about eight. The boy said, "Hi, mister."

"Wait in the kitchen," said the woman. "Please, darling, wait there and close the door." She hustled the children out of the hall and then came back to Port.

"Mrs. Simmon," said Port, "I apologize if I have alarmed you. All I meant to say was that I knew your husband wasn't here because I saw him at the store when I passed there." Then he smiled at her but it did not make an impression. She was hostile.

"If you're selling something, please leave. I don't let strangers—"

"I know you and I are strangers. I have your name from a friend. When he heard I was coming through here . . ."

"I don't care what you're selling, but if you don't leave right this minute—"

"I'm not selling anything. But that's why I carried my bag. Anyone seeing me would think the way you did. That I'm selling something."

He had said the wrong thing because she turned on her heels and went to the phone that hung on the wall.

"Was your maiden name Tomlin? Eve Tomlin?"

She reacted quickly and angrily. "What do you want? You want to make trouble? Are you somebody that—"

"Can we sit down somewhere, Mrs. Simmon? I can tell you much faster."

Then he saw that he had lost her. She was controlled now, and whatever it had been that had upset her did not matter too much anymore. So Port said, "I'm to give you regards from Abe Dalton."

Port saw that now she would sit down and hear him out, but she would do it out of fear and dislike. It would make the rest harder.

## Chapter 14

Eve Simmon sat in the chair at one side of the window and Port sat in the chair at the other. Eve looked as neat as the room. Her housedress was a catalog model with a small flowered print. The waves in her hair did not look like her own, and her hands were reddish from working with soap. She looked like most of the women in town.

If she were not so frightened, Port thought, or so hostile, her face would be pleasant.

"If you and Abe Dalton have some kind of trouble making in mind," she said, "don't think you're going to get away with anything. You sit right there all you want and when my husband comes home . . ."

"I'll leave now, if you want me to," Port told her. "I didn't think you would act this way." But he didn't move.

"Act what way?" she said, and sounded defensive.

"Angry about something. Did Abe ever harm you?"

She said nothing.

"He's sick. He may not get well. He just sends his regards."

She was still suspicious. "Don't tell me," she said. "Don't tell me you stopped in this town just to bring regards. I haven't seen him in—I don't know—it must be fifteen years." The thought made her remember. She had not intended that. "How old is he now, anyway?" Her voice sounded sharp again.

"He's very old, because of the things that have happened to him."

"I don't want to know anything about him."

She was in her early thirties, Port thought. She had

put on some weight but she was a firm-skinned woman and her face could be pleasant. But she tried too hard to be prim. It took away her attractiveness.

"Mrs. Simmon," said Port. "I'd like to try to convince you that nobody means you any harm. Abe Dalton, I told you, is a sick man. He's in a hospital now. He doesn't want anything that could—"

"He's a criminal, isn't he? And you know him, so maybe you're one of them too. Or a lawyer. That's just as bad."

"*You* know him," Port said. "Does that make you a criminal?"

She caught her breath and jumped out of the chair. "I'm a married woman with a home and children! My husband has a good business here and we have standing in our town. We have nothing but friends in this town, and my children—"

"Someone's coming," said Port. The car that had stopped in the drive was a delivery truck but the sign on the side of it read *Simmon Hardware*. The man that jumped out of the cab was no delivery boy. He was big and blond and he laughed when two of the children ran toward him from the house. He grabbed the small girl and threw her up in the air and when he had caught her again he came straight into the house.

"Eve?" he yelled from the stairs. "You home, honey?"

Eve Simmon turned pale.

"Sit still. I'm a salesman." Port was bent over, busy with the catch of his bag when the door swung open and the man came in.

He had started to say, "Eve, honey" again when he saw Port. "Oh—" He put the small girl down on the floor and closed the door. Then his smile came back and he said, "I'm Jay Simmon. How are you," and came across the room with his hand out.

"How are you, Mr. Simmon? My name's Port. I don't mean to disturb you—"

"That's all right; you're not." Jay Simmon looked down at the bag. "You trying to sell my wife something?" He laughed. "I bet I know what happened!"

Port laughed too, and said, "Yes, I'm afraid you're right. Well, if you'll excuse me—" but nobody was listening to him. Jay Simmon was asking his wife if she'd seen the A.O. Smith catalog and Eve Simmon got up to show him where he had left it on the hall table. They all came out to the hall and Port was just at the door.

"Hey—uh, Port, wasn't it?"

"Yes?"

"Give you a lift? I'm leaving too."

"No, thanks, I'm just going to the hotel."

"Come on," said Jay Simmon. "I used to be on the road myself. I know how the feet feel this time of day." He kissed his wife, waved at the children, and ran after Port.

Port didn't argue. He felt tired, but he didn't care one way or another about walking or riding. He sat next to Jay Simmon in the truck, holding his bag on his knees. Simmon backed out and headed down the street.

"What are you selling?" he said in a friendly voice.

Port shrugged, wishing he were alone. "Why should I talk to the competition?"

"I bet I can guess. Can openers."

"Yes," said Port. "You're right."

"Business good?"

Port shook his head.

"Know how I guessed? By your looks. Next to encyclopedias there's no line makes a man look so discouraged at the end of the day as can openers. Why'nt you try something else? I myself can undersell any gadget you got to peddle. You're in the wrong line."

"I know that," said Port. "I get off here."

"You're not offended, are you?" Jay Simmon looked closely into Port's face. "Because all I meant was some friendly—"

"I know that," said Port. "And thanks for the lift."

That night Port sat at the window and looked out over the town. Soon after nine the town seemed deserted and most of the lights on the main street went off. Port lay down on the bed, but he could not sleep. He had slept too much on the train. He felt uneasy about walking into Eve Simmon's safe little world. And if he left her alone and went back to the old man, who was dying anyway— Port started to smoke. He smoked three cigarettes and then he got up and stood by the window. There was nothing to see. He could not do any harm to Eve Simmon which her safe little world wouldn't mend. But the old man, Dalton, had nothing. He should be allowed to die as he wanted.

Port undressed and slept until morning.

At nine Port walked into Simmon's hardware store and asked for Jay. Jay was in the yard, stacking drain tiles. When he saw Port he came over and shook hands again.

"Hi, Port. Feeling better today? I hope you didn't think . . . Fact is, I was hoping you'd drop by or I'd run into you before you left."

"Good," said Port. "I was hoping—"

"I was thinking," Jay said without listening to Port, "that you might be interested in a proposition."

Port waited.

"You know anything about windmill pumps? No? Simple. Look, I need a man who goes out on the road—"

"Jay, I'm sorry. But I don't think—"

"You know what this job needs, mostly? A presentable guy, a guy that likes people, with—you know—appeal. You got that, Port. And if—"

"Jay, look, that's damn nice of you, but the fact is I have other obligations. The reason I'm here is that it seems I left one of my sample boards at your place. Did your wife find it, or say anything?"

"No."

"Can I run over to your house and check? I thought I'd ask you first . . ."

Jay laughed. "Sure, go on over. And tell her I said it's all right for you to come in." He grinned at Port. "You thought maybe she wouldn't, huh?"

"Frankly, yes," said Port. "And thank you again."

"Why don't you think over—"

Port said he would. He said that it was damn white of Jay to make the offer and that he'd think it over. Then he left and walked down Main Street to Elm, and all the way to Eve Simmon's house he was strangely comforted by the fact that he would always remember that once a man had offered him a job selling windmills to ranchers.

He rang the bell and heard Eve's steps in the hall. She opened the door without hesitation.

"My husband called me," she said. "You were coming over to pick up some samples you left here."

"Did you play it that way on the phone?"

"I don't intend having you mess up anything for me. Or for my husband." She held the door, waiting for Port to come in. She held it without welcome.

"I have said nothing to you that could make you think I want to mess up things for you," said Port. He went into the hall and when she had closed the door he followed her to the kitchen.

"You keep coming back," she said. "You must want something."

She was at the sink now, washing dishes, acting as if he weren't there.

"Where are the children?" asked Port.

She nodded out of the window. The little girl sat in the yard, patting her hands into the grass. The young boy was there, and an older one; they were painting a box.

"I'll tell you what I want and then I'll leave you alone. I can leave town tonight."

She washed dishes, waiting now.

"Abe Dalton just got out of prison. He's sick, and he's old. I told you that."

She kept washing with a slow, rotating motion.

"There's somebody who wants him to do one more job, and than another, and another. You know how it is with blackmailers."

"Not until now," she said tonelessly.

"The pressure on Dalton is an old job, a bank that was knocked over. He didn't do it, but it looks as if he did."

She was still washing the same dish without looking at it.

"He didn't do that job. He was with you."

Except for the slow, rotating motion she did not move.

"It can send Abe back to prison. He'll die there," said Port.

The circle of her movement over the dish got smaller.

"You can help him, Mrs. Simmon. You need not be involved, no one here need find out, and if your statement does become necessary—"

Port saw that she had stopped moving now.

"Mrs. Simmon," he said. "Do you hate him?"

She said it very low and fast, almost in a whisper.

"You don't know what I have here, you don't know

how much. I won't give it up. You come into all this and drag back every rotten thing I thought was buried!" Suddenly she turned toward Port and her wet hands hung at her sides, dripping water on the clean floor. Her face had a high color now and Port saw that she was close to tears. "You don't know how I met him, do you? You don't know how it used to be, who little Eve Tomlin used to be, do you? He knew my father. Abe Dalton was on the lam, and he knew my father. We lived out on a farm, in the bluff country where nothing's any good except that you're alone. He knew my father who was a drunk and a filthy thief and a crooked old man who always kept talking about the great times and the big deals he used to have in the city—a long time ago when he used to leave Mother and me alone out there and toot off to some city and come back broke and ragged. And when Mother died he really showed what he was, drinking and cursing and me in the middle of it, and then he had friends over—"

The tears were running down over her cheeks now but she didn't notice them.

"Friends, he used to call them, big-time friends from the big days in the city. They were crooks hiding out and they paid him for it and that's all that filthy old man ever cared about because that's how he bought his liquor. He'd sit in the kitchen all night talking to himself and to the bottle because his 'friend' got the one bedroom, the one with the double bed, because the bed I used to sleep on was too narrow for two, and when that filthy old drunk was ready to pass out he'd use my bed because I wasn't using it then."

She shook her hands violently, making the water spray off them.

"That's how I met Dalton, you understand? I was less than twenty and Abe Dalton was a stranger who came, stayed a while, and had bed and board. You understand?" Her voice got high with excitement. "He was as old as my father, almost, and a stranger! I don't want to talk any more. I don't want to think any more!"

Then she was silent. She turned away from Port and he was glad that she did because it was easier for him, not knowing what to say. He saw her shoulders move when she took a deep breath and then she stood still again. Port put his hands in his pockets and he had an urge to whistle, softly and for the short time it took him to see clearly again.

He said, "I'm glad you made it. And no one will take it away from you."

She went to the refrigerator and took out a bottle of milk. She carried it over to the stove and poured some into a pot.

"You made it, Mrs. Simmon. Dalton didn't." He waited a moment. "Do you remember him well enough to know that he wouldn't take anything from you?"

Port could not see her face because she had turned to the stove and was watching the milk she was heating.

"Isn't there anything you remember of him that wasn't bad?"

She went to a cupboard and took out a bottle. She gave Port one brief look but he couldn't tell what the look meant. Then she went back to the stove and poured milk into the bottle.

"You married a very short time after Dalton knew you. Perhaps that way you can remember about him. What I'm trying to make you see, Mrs. Simmon—"

"I remember."

The words were unexpected, and the tone of her voice was unexpected. It was as if she were no longer fighting it off, the time in the past, but was really thinking about it now.

"I remember because he was the last." She looked at Port. "He didn't tell you?"

"He didn't want me to come," said Port. "He just told me your name."

She put a nipple on the neck of the bottle but she didn't look away from Port.

"He took me with him," she said. "The night he left." She went to the window and looked out at her children. "My father was asleep in the kitchen—or passed out, I don't know which. Abe Dalton drove me to Grand Rapids, driving all that night and part of the next day. In Grand Rapids he found me a room. I must have been half dead with fear and excitement because I went to sleep as soon as we got there." She turned back to Port. "When I woke up he was gone. It was terrible being alone there. I must have cried myself to sleep again. That's why I didn't find it until I woke up the next morning. He had put five hundred dollars in my shoe."

Port said nothing when she was finished. He smiled at her briefly. It looked for a moment as if she were going to smile back but then she didn't. She looked down at the bottle and felt it for warmth.

"I know," she said. "This is all good. It's good as long as Jay doesn't know. I met him very soon afterwards and he never knew about me."

"Don't you think . . ."

She didn't let Port finish. "He was from Otter Bend, but we had already known each other. We went back to Otter Bend very soon. We were married in the city and went back to Otter Bend, and it was as if I'd never seen the town before. This is my life now, and Jay will never know."

"You won't help Dalton?" said Port.

"You can force me," she said, "and ruin everything." She sounded almost indifferent. "And I would try to fight back."

She was at the window again looking out at the baby, so she didn't see Port frown.

"Jay doesn't know, and he never will." She went to the door that led out to the yard. "I must get my baby," she said and went out.

When she came back Port was gone.

She seemed very calm the rest of the day, and during the evening when her husband was home. She talked very little. Jay Simmon noticed this but he said nothing of it. When they went to bed he fell asleep quickly.

Eve Simmon lay awake for a long time and when she got up it was barely light. She went downstairs to the small desk in the living room. She sat there over a blank sheet of paper with pen in her hand. The sheet had a letterhead, *Mrs. Jay Simmon,* and Eve Simmon read it several times. Then she wrote her name, *Mrs. Jay Simmon.* She wrote it again, automatically, because she did not want to sit at the desk, with pen and paper, and do nothing at all.

Jay's truck was outside, under the window, and a swing in the yard was swaying in the cold morning wind.

She tried to write again. She wrote Mrs. Jay Simmon,

over and over. She felt like crying, but she fought it.

"Eve?" Jay called from upstairs.

"Honey?" he called again.

She got up and went to the stairs. "Yes, Jay?"

He came downstairs, big and rumpled from sleep. "You all right, honey?"

She nodded.

"No, you're not," he said. "Come on out to the kitchen. I'll make us some coffee."

He put the coffee on and then sat down at the kitchen table with her.

"Like before we had the kids, huh, Eve?"

She nodded and almost smiled.

"Honey," he said. "You want me to leave you alone?"

This time she did cry. She could not hold it back. Jay Simmon put his arms around his wife and pulled her up. He patted her head and stroked her back.

She relaxed after a while but did not let him go. They went back upstairs that way to their bed, and they made love the way she remembered before she had had any children.

She had not talked at all. She said nothing about it, ever.

## *Chapter 15*

LETTY was a sound sleeper, but when the bright light hit her face she woke up almost immediately. She sat up, more to get the glare from the ceiling out of her eyes than for any other reason. Then she saw Dicky standing in the door and came awake all the way.

"Dicky! You're back!" she said and smiled with her whole face. Then she threw back the covers and watched him come over to the bed. "You're back so soon," she said, smiling again.

She didn't see it coming but she heard him say, "Bitch!" and then the pain stung into her face and she fell sideways.

When she tried to get up out of the bed he hit her again, harder.

She could not think at all. She stayed curled on the bed at first, and then, when nothing else happened, she let the weakness come over her. She stayed there with the sheets rumpled around her and felt the burning on her face and a pain like a sharp singing inside her ear.

"Get some clothes on," she heard him say. "We got company." When she did not move immediately he snapped, "Get decent, you bitch!"

She sat up quickly, afraid he would hit her again. Dicky threw the bathrobe at her. It hit her in the face and wrapped itself halfway around her neck.

"Come on, come on—"

She put the robe on as fast as she could and when she had it tied securely Dicky went to the door and said, "It's all right now. You can come in."

Mac came in. He nodded at her but he didn't really look at her. He let his eyes wander along the walls and the floor.

"Get something going on that hotplate," said Dicky. "I been driving all night."

"Coffee?"

"What else, lamebrain?"

The two men sat down at the table while Letty started the coffee. They lit cigarettes and Mac said they really made time coming in and Dicky said yes, and wait till I put in that new carburator but what he'd like to do best of all was to get one of those special transmissions, like the kind they had been talking about. Then he turned in his chair and watched Letty. She could feel his stare on her back.

"Come here, bitch," he said.

Letty turned around. She did not look sleepy and her eyes were much smaller than usual.

"Dicky, I don't want—"

"Shut up!" he said very loudly. "I'm talking, and you listen. Didn't think I'd be back this soon, did you? And as soon as I turn my back you think you can play the field?" His voice rose on a moral note. "I dress you up! I feed you to keep you in shape! I put a roof over your head and a bed under your rear and all you ever give back is what you give out for free anyway! I don't buy that, lamebrain! I don't go for that one little bit—" He gasped, almost choking himself. "And on top of that with a son of a bitch like Port! The first day I'm out of town shacking up with that—"

"Dicky!"

"I'm talking!"

"Dicky! You're wrong. I didn't do any such thing. What I was doing—".

"You calling my friend here a liar?" Dicky was out of his chair.

Letty stared at Mac. She didn't know what to say. Mac looked back at her, his face hurt yet mild, and Letty could think of nothing to say.

"The water's boiling. Let's have that coffee," Dicky grunted.

"Dicky. Will you listen to me, please?"

He got off his chair again and stepped very close to her.

"You want me to mark you up? For real?"

Her face got very still. "I'm leaving," she said.

"The hell you're leaving."

"Let go my arm, Dicky."

"Mac," Dicky said over his shoulder. "Shall I mark her up?"

"Naw. Don't mark her up." Mac looked at his cigarette.

"You still leaving?" Dicky asked her.

She did not answer.

"You wanna go join that Port bastard somewheres?" She looked stubborn.

"You wanna tell me where he went?"

His grip on her arm became more and more painful.

"He's coming back," said Mac. "She said so the first time."

"Shut up, Mac." Dicky put his face close to Letty's. "He coming back after you?"

"You're wasting time, Dicky," said Mac. "We got things to do. If he comes back."

"Yeah." Dicky let go of her arm. "Get that coffee going."

"I'm leaving," she said.

"You stay till I tell you different," said Dicky. He gave her a violent shove that sent her flying back and over the bed. The shock showed in her face and she didn't try to get up. She lay there and made no sound.

"To hell with the coffee," said Dicky. He turned off the

heat under the pot and went to the closet. "I'll be maybe two hours." He reached for a suit.

"You'll be?" said Mac. "You going alone?"

"This thing needs the right clothes," said Dicky. "Lookit you, with that rainbow shirt and the jacket."

Dicky shook out the suit he had in his hand and then started to change his clothes.

"What time, Mac?"

"Just past seven."

"Crap. I can't get in there till eight."

"Better go early just the same. Maybe you can figure more than one way."

"Sure," said Dicky. He was pulling his pants on. "Two, three hours," he said. "I'll meet you here."

Mac nodded and looked at the tip of his cigarette.

"I don't want her to leave," said Dicky and jerked his head at the bed.

"Sure," said Mac.

Letty sat up on the bed. Her eyes were wide and she wanted to say something.

"Shut up and keep still," said Dicky. "Or I'll mark you up."

"Don't mark her up," said Mac.

Letty sat where she was. Her hair slid down over the side of her face and she reached up to push it back. Dicky slammed the door shut behind him. She bent her head which made her hair slide down again.

Then she saw Mac's feet by the bed. She left her hair down the way it had fallen.

## Chapter 16

THERE was a fan over the long desk, and each time the fan swung through its cycle it blew a draft of medicinal odors over Port's face. The smell irritated him but if he moved he would lose his place in the line and if he had to stay there much longer he would be ready to insult the receptionist, once the old woman came his way. She was busy with forms, nodding and chatting with the man who sat in the visitor's chair by her desk.

"Maybe I'll drop to the floor and have a fit," said someone in the line behind Port. "Maybe then I'll get some attention."

"Don't kid yourself," said someone else. "In this clinic you got to be dead to get service."

"If you tell 'em you died, maybe."

"That old woman there, she's still here. And she's dead."

The old woman behind the reception desk finished with the visitor and swiveled around to look at the line. It pleased her to see such activity and to know that it was all coming her way. When she saw Port she smiled, because to remember a customer gave her a special pleasure.

"Mr. Port, wasn't it? From the parole board, isn't that right?" She reached for the pad she used for the passes.

She asked Port whom he was going to see, and Port told her the name and the floor and the ward. He got his pass, he got past the floor nurse, and he left his slip on the table at the door of the ward. The nurse who usually sat there was busy distributing pills.

It would not be easy to tell Dalton about Eve Simmon, but Port went down the length of the ward fast, because he had been away so long.

Dalton did not have the tubes going into his arm and his nose, and when Port got to the side of the bed he saw that the man asleep in the bed was not Abe Dalton.

Port bit his lip. He went back to the door, almost running, to speak to the nurse who was back at her desk now.

"Dalton? Abraham Dalton?" She checked in her book. She looked up once to give Port a stern glance because he had started to whistle.

"He's not here," she said.

"I know that. I want to know where is is!"

"Would you mind keeping your voice—"

"Don't try humoring me, lady. Look it up. What happened to Dalton!"

She had to look in another book and, being offended, was awkward about it.

"Dalton! D-a-l-t—"

"Oh, him," she said. "Yes, he's been discharged."

"Discharged? He walked out of here?"

"We don't call it *discharged* when they're deceased," said the nurse huffily.

For a moment Port let the relief sweep through him and he could feel the tension go out of his muscles. The nurse was talking again.

"There was some question about the matter, but there's nothing we can do in a case like that."

"What? What case?"

"The patient leaving. The resident had to sign him out but warned him, of course, to get back into bed. And to consult a physician."

"You let him go? Didn't he—"

"He paid his bill," said the nurse. "The young man paid the bill."

Port held very still for a moment. He wet his lips and said slowly, "This young man. Sort of short, muscular type? Black hair with a wave in it?"

"You know him?"

Port left without another word. He had made the mistake of leaving Dalton alone, the mistake of chasing after Eve Simmon, and the mistake of treating Corday like a human being.

He took a cab to Dalton's place. The landlady said Dalton hadn't been in for almost a week, and his rent was due. Port gave her two weeks' rent and left. He took another cab to Dicky's hotel, sitting with his arms on the driver's back rest staring out of the window. He didn't say a word.

"Look," the cabby said. "I can't go any faster—"

"I didn't ask you to. Just drive."

The cabby didn't say anything more. He could feel his customer's mood. It was a mood that hung over his shoulder like a gun with the hair trigger cocked.

"Here it is," said the cabby. "Here's the hotel." The cab rolled up to the curb.

The back door to the cab was half open already.

"One-twenty-five," said the cabby but Port had a bill out by then and let it fall on the driver's seat.

"Count it later," he said and was gone.

He went past the desk and the clerk looked up, opened his mouth, and shut it again. At the door to Dicky's room Port knocked once and walked in.

There were clothes strewn over a chair, two cups and a jar of coffee on the table. The cups were clean.

It was late afternoon. Letty was still in bed.

"Letty—you awake?"

She turned her head toward him but the rest of her stayed toward the wall.

"Letty! Snap out of it."

The bed sheet was twisted around one of her legs and the blanket was mostly bunched over her hips. She was wearing a nightgown.

"Come on, girl. Whatever it was, it's over. Up with you." Port gave her a boost by one arm.

She wasn't drunk, Port saw, and she wasn't tired, but she was down to a key where nothing could trouble her much.

"Was Dicky here? Letty!"

"He's gone."

"Was Dalton with him? Letty, answer me!"

She let herself drop back onto the bed and turned to the wall. She mumbled something but Port didn't catch it. He tried again but she wouldn't answer. She shook his hand off her shoulder when he tried to turn her around. He decided to give her a chance to recover from whatever it had been.

"Letty, get up now, come on, girl." He helped her up again, but this time he held her arm and led her across the room. "Now you go in there and take a shower. I'll turn it on for you. You like it hot? Medium? Never mind, I'll set it the way it should be." He adjusted the taps and arranged the curtain so that the water wouldn't spray out. "Now get in there and—Christ, take that shirt off first. All right, take your shower, then get dressed, and meanwhile I'll make you some coffee. All right?"

She nodded and started to pull off her nightgown before Port was out of the door.

He boiled the water that was on the hotplate and smoked a cigarette while he waited. The shower went off in the bathroom and Letty stuck her head out of the door. She was still wet.

"Will you hand me my clothes?" she said. "On the closet door. Inside."

Port gave her the clothes and then waited some more, pacing back and forth, whistling low, and tonelessly.

She came into the room, dressed, with a towel wrapped around her wet hair. A hank of it showed over the green towel, and Port noticed how blonde her hair could look.

"Here's yours," said Port and handed her a cup of hot water mixed with instant coffee. He fixed his own, sat down and said, "You act as if Dicky ran out on you."

"I don't like him any more." Her tone was flat.

"The same," said Port. He was bent over, sipping coffee, so he didn't see the look she gave him. When he lifted his head she was looking elsewhere.

"You think so?" she said.

She had been hurt, Port thought. She looked very quiet. She didn't seem to care very much, and Port felt he would have to go slowly. She might help, but he would have to watch her.

"Where is Dicky?" Port asked.

"He left. He went to Newton."

The long trip to Otter Bend, the careful handling of Eve Simmon, the waiting for Letty—that was over now.

"Where is Abe Dalton?"

"He went—Dicky took him along."

"To do a job?"

"Yes."

"When?"

"Soon. I don't know when."

"How sick was Dalton? Did he walk, eat—"

"He wasn't here long. He didn't look good, but he got around."

"He's going to be in on that job in person?"

"Dicky said yes, and Dalton didn't argue long. He just said to wait two more days—two anyway—so he'd have his strength back."

"And Dicky said?"

"He said okay. He had to say okay. Dalton made that very clear. Dalton can get that way, I guess. Besides, he was so weak they could see it."

"Corday and Dalton are going to pull this alone?"

"And two more. Mac and Loony."

"Mac? You know this Mac?"

"Yes," she said. "I know this Mac."

"He does what?"

"I don't know. Wheel man, I think."

"And Loony? That's the machinist guy, isn't he?"

"Loony's there now. Dicky left him there."

"You know what he does?"

"I don't know. He's got himself hired at the plant and he's working there. That's why Dicky and him went there in the first place. To find out more things about everything there."

"And they left when—with Dalton, I mean?"

"Today. Before noon."

"Today," said Port. "Today is Monday. The money is there on Thursday night."

Port looked down at his cup. Then he clinked his fingernail against the side of the cup. "Monday, Tuesday, Wednesday," he said. "Monday, Tuesday, Wednesday."

Letty got up and brought back the pot of water. She put more coffee powder in both of the cups and then poured water over it. Port was still clinking his fingernail against the rim of his cup and as the water ran into the cup the sound changed, getting flatter and harder. Then he got up and went to the window.

It was getting dark outside and the hotel sign had come on, going blink, blink, blink.

"Letty." Port turned and looked at her. "You going to help?"

She shrugged. "I tried helping you once before."

"What happened wasn't your fault."

"I know. That's what I mean."

Port came back to the table and stood beside Letty. He understood that she meant something other than not having helped enough with the information she had gotten at the pool room.

"What, Letty? Tell me."

Her face got sullen and she turned her head so that he could not see it. He put his hand on her shoulder and said, "What, Letty."

"I'm disappointed," she said.

Port did not ask any more. She had told him what was important.

Then Port walked around so he could see her. He said, "If this works, Letty, what happened to you needn't happen again."

He wanted to say something else but she didn't let him finish.

"I'll help you," she said. "What is it?"

He pulled his chair close to hers and then talked. It was clear and very impersonal.

"You have any money?"

"No."

He gave her money.

"You know where Dalton lives?"

"No."

"I'll take you there later. I want you out of here."

She nodded.

"I want you to stay there for twenty-four hours. There's a phone in the hall outside his room. I'll need to call you."

She nodded.

"You want to know what I'm going to do?"

"No."

"You don't care about Dicky?"

"I don't care."

"Just as well."

They left and Port took her to Dalton's room. Since Port had just paid the landlady her rent the landlady didn't care, so Letty took over the room without any trouble. Port left immediately.

It was now eight in the evening, and he did not have much time.

## *Chapter 17*

PORT called a man whom he had never met, but that didn't matter too much. They both knew of each other. Port reached the man at his home, a legitimate home with a listed number, because most men like him had legitimate fronts. The conversation was short.

"I'm Port. Daniel Port. I'm in town and I need some advice."

"Who did you say? You're who?"

"Stop horsing around. You know I'm in town."

"I know Port's in town. We keep track."

"What I need—"

"How do I know you're him?"

"Because I know you."

"So do the cops."

"Do they know you put Cassman in office? Do they know you're up to your neck in a thing with the liquor commission—"

"Shut up! Christ, shut up on the phone!"

"So who am I?"

"All right, so you're Port. Christ, you sound like him. Nobody else would have the gall to—"

"Here's what I need."

"Listen, if you're gonna stir up—"

"It's nothing. You're just the only one I know of in town, and I need a small hand."

"What? If this is—"

"Shut up and listen, all right?"

"All right."

"I've got to see a pawnbroker big enough to carry some value. Not a fence, a legitimate pawnbroker. But he's got to be willing to play some ball."

"How you gonna find a legitimate anything that's—"

"What's the matter with you in this town? Haven't you got a man that looks clean but you know about him?"

"That's all you want? A pawnbroker like that?"

"Who?"

"Schneider on Ninth. Corner Ninth and Commercial."

"Call him and tell him I'm coming. And tell him to hear me out."

"All right. If that's all."

"One more thing. You know anybody on the local paper?"

"Sure. Who?"

"Somebody who'll do you a favor about what to print and how big."

"Listen, Port. This paper we got here in town is clean almost all the way through. This town's proud to have—"

"Stop it, stop it. I'll get sick. All I want is a boost on some news. Local news. Can you get it some space?"

"If it's got anything to do with cleaning up this town, I can maybe get the night desk to shuffle the space. Anything to do with cleaning up—"

"You said that. I'll have Schneider call you back. He'll tell you when it's time to plug the news."

"What news?"

"Schneider will tell you."

"If that's all—"

"That's all. No strain, was it? So long."

"Hey! Wait—"

"What?"

"You leaving town, Port?"

"You're so big you don't know?" Port hung up in the middle of the other man's cursing.

He took a taxi to Ninth and Commercial and walked into Schneider's just before closing time.

For a pawnshop Schneider's place had a look of elegance. Bright lights made the choice pieces of jewelry sparkle in the long glass cases, and the cabinets with musical instruments on the right and optical instruments on the left were arranged neatly and with an eye for display. Nothing was crowded and there was no junk. Port ignored the two salesmen and walked to the cage in back. There was a small, worried man sitting there.

"Are you Schneider?" said Port.

"Yes. But we're closing. If you want—"

"I'm Daniel Port. You're expecting me."

The small man looked even more worried and ran his hand over his bald skull. "Yes, yes," he said without looking up. "This way, please. There's a table. We can sit at this table—"

Port came around to the back where Schneider had a place fixed up for making loan applications. Schneider was at the desk already, but Port didn't sit down.

"Let me look around first."

"Around? You mean here?" Schneider ran his hand over his skull again.

"Just to look around."

He looked around, and then he sat down at the table and he and Schneider had a detailed talk. It lasted until after closing, and when Port left he did so by the back door.

It was ten now. Port had a drink at a bar, looked in on Letty, saw that she was fine, went to Dicky's hotel and left there in a very short time. He killed time until twelve, and in one of the neighborhood bars he made a point of finding out what Loony's real name was. Then he checked once more with the man whom he knew in this town. After that Port went to sleep.

He left town very early in the morning in a rented car. There were street-cleaning machines making rounds through the empty city, and milkmen and paper boys. At a corner where the light was red, Port bought the morning edition from a boy. He glanced at the first page and at the second but when the light changed he took off immediately. Further out he bought a bottle of milk from a wagon because he had not found any restaurants open. Once on the highway he drove very fast. He took the cap off the bottle and drank some milk. It was very cold and without taste. He drank some more and then let the bottle fly into a ditch. He rolled up the window again. He was smiling. He was smiling about something else.

## *Chapter 18*

NEWTON was a small town with pretensions toward a kind of cozy age. There were store fronts with casement windows and leaded windows, and trim fences outside the houses. Almost everybody belonged to the big happy fake family that worked for the Newton Tool and Die Works.

The plant was out at the edge of town, home-owned, home-managed, and home-staffed. The gate was built like a bastion, though the plant wasn't very old—or was the Newton family. There was a statue on the town square, not of the usual Civil War soldier but of Sherman Newton, who was still alive and running his plant.

The plant had no gatehouse. You could walk into the yard without being stopped. There were no signs saying admittance to personnel only and there were no numbers on the various buildings. The one visible sign said *Enter*. Port entered, looking for the employment office where they could tell him how to find Kostanovitch, which was Loony's last name.

Port walked into a long room with a ramp. On one side of the ramp were three time clocks, and on the other side was an old lady, wearing celluloid cuffs buttoned over her wrists.

"May I help you, sir?" She sounded nice and old-fashioned.

"I'm looking for the employment office," said Port.

"I'm the employment office." Then her face turned almost sad. "But it's almost five, sir. Wouldn't you like to come back tomorrow?"

"This won't take long. All I want to ask—"

"It's almost five, sir," she said again, but this time with an old-fashioned chiding sound.

"I know, but all—"

She smiled sadly and walked away from the ramp as if she didn't see anyone there. She went to her desk and started to dust.

Port sucked in his breath and held it for a moment.

It made a sound when he let out his breath and the old lady looked at him, but Port wasn't looking at her. Behind the casement windows lined with cute figurines converted into ivy plants Port saw the parking lot and the car. Dicky Corday had had the rear end lowered, the bumper moved back to make room for a spare, and lights, reflectors, and antennae added. Dalton could not be too well, or he wouldn't have let Corday show that car on the streets.

It was almost five, and the workers would be emerging at any moment. Port left without another word. At the door he heard the old lady call, "See you tomorrow—" as if they had a date.

Port sat in his car outside the gate. When the rush started, Port didn't worry about missing the car because there was only one like it in Newton. The car came out and headed for an across-the-tracks part of the town. It stopped in front of a three-story house with a patchy lawn in front. The house wasn't old-fashioned, it was just old. A man, big and blond, got out of the car, carrying a lunch bucket under his arm. That was Loony, Port thought. Loony lived here, and maybe the rest of them, too.

Port sat and smoked for a while. It was getting dark and nobody came in or out of the house. Port flipped his cigarette out onto the street but sat for a while longer. His hands were on the wheel and his thumbs rubbed slowly back and forth. He made a slow, breathy whistle in the same rhythm.

Finally Port stopped whistling. It was very dark and

very quiet inside the car. There was a small click when he opened the glove compartment but no sound at all when he dropped the revolver into his pocket. Then he went into the house.

Dicky would be the kind to take a room way up on top. It would feel out of the way to him and much safer. Dalton would take a room on the bottom. It would attract no more or no less attention and it would be easier to get out fast.

Port tried the downstairs first.

The landlady's apartment had a sign on the door—*Day, Week, or Month. No Pets or Children.* The door next to it was open, but there wasn't even any funiture inside the room. Port roamed down the hall until he saw a door in front of which were six empty milk bottles. Port almost knocked one of them over. No pets or children, and six bottles of milk? Port listened at the door and he heard, ". . . so then I put the screw end in the turntable and . . ."

"Loony, please! I don't give a damn if you turned a screw or screwed a tern."

"That boy loves his work," said somebody else. "Always jamming about screws, grinders, Brigeports."

"Bridgeports," said Loony. "That's a machine what—"

"I'm telling you, this keeps up and you can stay on that job. We get done here you can stay in this Newton burg and work permanent!"

"I may do that! I may just do that," said Loony. "It's a good job. And very—sort of— old-fashioned, you could call it. I might just—"

"All right!"

That was Dicky Corday. And then there was Loony and somebody else. Mac, the one Letty didn't seem to like. If Dalton were there, he wasn't talking. Perhaps he was too sick.

Port turned the door handle and entered the room almost in one movement. He closed the door behind him so quietly that the men in the room had barely focused on him.

"All around," said Port. "Sit still."

Dicky jumped up and then stopped because Port was showing the gun. The little black hole looked steady and large to Dicky. For a moment they all stared at the gun in

Port's hand, staring and letting his presence sink in.

Port saw Dalton standing at the far end of the room. The old man had been stirring something in a pot. He didn't seem to know what to do with his spoon.

"Don't let it burn," said Port. He was grinning. Then he turned back to the others because they were coming to life.

"I came for two things. Abe Dalton, and Abe Dalton's notes."

"Whatcha gonna do?" said Mac. "Shoot everybody?"

"Shut up," said Dicky.

"No, I mean it," Mac said. "You got an idea this is some kinda Western?"

"Listen to Corday," said Port. He didn't like Mac, and it showed. "Listen to him and this'll be short." His voice was quiet. "I can make this long, if you want."

Mac looked at Loony without turning his head. "Rush him!" he said suddenly.

Loony didn't move. He stood near the table, the lunch bucket still in his hands. He didn't know what to do with it. Then he said, "Can I sit down?"

Port nodded and watched Loony sit down.

"Loony—" Mac started again.

"You running this?" Port looked at Dicky.

"Dicky," said Mac, and his voice sounded almost uninterested. "Ain't he the one who took over your dame?"

The needle worked.

"Let's see you ain't bluffing," said Dicky. He was sweating, and a slow flush crept under his skin. "You think you're so hot—"

"He's bluffing," said Mac. "I can tell. Here!" He moved quickly, as if reaching for something to throw at Port. Port only moved the gun in a small arc. He moved his mouth too, and Mac got the impression that Port was going to whistle. Mac got confused. He had to do something else.

"A slow one, ain'tcha?" He laughed. "Speaking of slow, has Letty—"

He let it drop when he saw Port begin to move. Port walked toward Mac.

"You're bluffing—" said Mac.

Port came closer. Mac was unable to laugh, but he managed a grin. He held the grin and tried outstaring

Port. He still had his eyes wide open when the gunsight cut through his nose.

First he trembled and then he fell to the floor. He lay there holding his face and breathing in sharp gusts.

"I'm sick of that guy," said Port. "I get sick enough, Corday, and I do worse!"

But Dicky hardly heard. His rage burst out, raw and ugly.

"You son of a bitch—you stinking son of a bitch! I'm gonna get you if it takes from now till hell! I hate your guts worse than anyone that ever crossed me up and nobody crosses me up, nobody's gonna keep—"

"Stop dreaming and listen."

"I'll get you! I'll frame you up and then I'll step on you! You think squeezing Dalton was something? You think squeezing Dalton was the best can be done? Lemme tell you what's gonna—"

"Here!" Port reached into his pocket and pulled out a newspaper. He tossed it on the table where Dicky could reach it. "Here, Corday. Lemme show *you* how it's done!"

Dicky stopped shouting.

"Read it," said Port. "The column on the right about routine crime and routine pursuit."

It meant nothing to Dicky but it held his attention. He picked up the paper.

"First and second paragraph is all you need. The rest is just the same thing all over." Port's gun tapped the column. "Read." The last tap was sharp and tore the paper, and then the gun pointed at Dicky again. Dicky read:

> Our police, like any large institutional body, need the occasional bite of public criticism. This column is meant to furnish that bite.

"Keep reading," said Port.

> Maybe it's routine for a thief to make a living off the efforts of others—that's his crime. Does that justify the crime of routine on the part of a lethargic police force which contents itself with filing a complaint, stacking it away by hour and alphabet, and then—if the man can be spared—sending out a disinterested employee to see if the crime really occurred?

"Did you come to the part about Schneider?" said Port.

Dicky looked up, impatient. The prose made him feel stupid and he had lost interest.

"I know it's an effort," said Port. "But it may save your skin. Read."

> Schneider's Pawnshop was robbed of five thousand dollars in cash and twenty-five thousand dollars in jewelry. Of course, it wasn't jewelry stolen from the home of a leading citizen—just from Schneider's pawnshop. Maybe that isn't enough of an incentive for the police to . . .

"You seen the part about Schneider?"

"Yeah," said Dicky. "I can read."

"What's it say?"

"He was robbed. Twenty-five grand hard and five cash."

"What else?"

"The cops are getting the needle."

"Don't bother reading the rest. They really get it by the time it's over."

"I'm worried," said Dicky. "I'm already shaking."

"The guy who pulled that heist is worried," Port said. "It's going to be as tough as if he stole the queen's garter."

"I'm shaking," said Dicky.

"You should. That fall guy is you!"

Dalton had long since stopped stirring his pot. He was now standing near Mac, who was still lying on the floor, curled into a ball. At Port's last words there was such a deep silence in the room that Mac turned slowly to look up. No one moved and no one made sound.

The tableau held for a long moment. Then Dicky Corday started to laugh, loudly and violently, until he was winded and had to stop. "Sucker bluff," he kept saying. "Sucker bluff—" He was hoarse now.

Port put the gun back into his pocket and said, "It's in your apartment."

"Huh?"

"The loot from the Schneider robbery. It's in your apartment. Robbery. I hear you've been up for the same thing once before. You know what the second offense carries in this state?"

Dicky stared at Port and turned pale.

"I guess you know," said Port. "So help me, Corday, I'll nail it on you. I made that frame so it won't come apart. It's over you, solid."

"No—"

"Yes. Unless you want to give me Dalton's notes." Then Port shrugged. "They wouldn't help you any after ten or twenty years in jail. How old are you now, in your thirties? When you get out you'll be just a little younger than Dalton, you know that?"

Dicky looked at Dalton and so did everyone else. Mac was sitting up on the floor, his hands cupped over his face. He looked up over his hands at Dalton. The old man turned away then, and went to the stove.

"All right, Corday. Make up your mind," Port said.

"How do I know—"

"You don't—if you want to end up in stir."

"How do I know you—you'll trade even? The frame I got on Dalton for the frame you got on me?"

"You got a phone?" Port asked.

"There's one at the end of the hall," said Loony.

Port took the gun out of his pocket and nodded at Dalton. "Hold this. Loony can sit at the table and Mac should stay on the floor."

"All right," said Dalton, and took the gun.

Corday and Port went to the end of the hall.

"You got any silver?" asked Port.

Dicky was too nervous to argue now. He handed Port some change and Port dialed long distance.

Corday began to suck his teeth. Then he shifted his weight from one foot to the other, looked at the cracks in the wall, and avoided turning in Port's direction. His brain was going frantically, but it solved nothing for him and made him feel tired.

"Corday."

He turned almost with a jerk, and saw Port with the phone to his ear. "Better listen to this," said Port and then he spoke into the phone. "This is Daniel Port," he said to Letty. "Can you hear me?"

She could hear him and Port went on, without using her name. Dicky heard only what Port was saying.

"Now listen close. Last night there was a robbery in town. Schneider's pawnshop. Yes, the one that got written up. Listen. The loot from the robbery is in Dicky Corday's hotel room. No. Leave it there. It's behind the small access door to the plumbing, that little door in the bathroom next to the sink. You know where I mean? Right. Now, here's what you do." Port looked at his watch. "What time do you have? Right, good enough. Here's what you do. If I don't call you back within fifteen minutes—fifteen minutes— you phone the police and tell them where they can find the loot from the Schneider robbery. Clear? You got it. Yes. Sure looks like it, doesn't it. All right now, you wait fifteen minutes. If I don't call, Corday is it." Port hung up.

He looked at Corday and said, "Made up your mind?"

## *Chapter 19*

THERE were only twelve minutes left and it showed on everyone. Port had stayed by the door, because that way he could get to the phone more quickly. Dalton was standing next to him. He was still holding the gun, making small, nervous arcs with it from Loony to Dicky, to Mac and then back to Loony again. Dalton did not want anything to go wrong. He wanted this to be over, to be able to lie down and to cover himself with a warm blanket.

Loony still sat at the table. The perspiration on his forehead made his blond hair damp at the edges, staining it dark. He was worried about Dicky. He was worried that Dicky might be crazy and do something wrong.

Mac had pushed himself up onto the couch. His breathing was careful and noisy. His nose was swollen and tight and crusted with dried blood. He blinked his eyes as if they were too dry or as if he had something in them.

"Ten minutes, Corday."

Port watched Dicky standing there where the four men could see him. Dicky seemed to be dying with indecision.

"Eight minutes," said Port. "And remember the four minutes it takes for the call. You now have less than five."

"Dicky," said Dalton. "Better give him the paper. He'll go through with it otherwise."

Finally Dicky spoke. He seemed to be almost pleading.

"How do I know? You keep saying he'll do this, he'll do that—how do I know the whole thing isn't—"

"Dan isn't that way," Dalton said. "That's all. I know him."

"You know him, you know him! How do *I* know—"

"I wouldn't deal with him," Dalton said, "if he were different."

Dicky knew one thing at least; that Dalton had always been straight. In Dalton's life there had always been that one island of honesty. It made his word good and it made him different from others who lived the way he had.

"You say so?" Dicky said.

"Don't you know me?" Dalton was no longer holding the gun on the room.

"A bargain's a bargain," said Dicky. "You say so."

"It's my word," said Dalton. Everyone knew it was so.

"Two minutes, and I phone." Port opened the door. He stood that way, holding the door, and watched Dicky Corday move fast now. Dicky pulled off his right shoe. He put it on top of the table and fumbled inside it until he had the thin leather out of the sole. He reached into the toe, pressing his hand into the shoe, and held up the folded papers. He looked as if he had been running.

"Put them on the table and open them up."

Dicky did that.

"Abe, take a look."

Dalton went to the table and looked at the papers.

"They're all here."

"Take them," said Port. "Corday?"

Dicky looked up, waiting. He was no longer trying to think. It would make no difference.

"You and me make a phone call."

Dicky and Port left the room and Port placed the call. Dicky was not nervous any more. He felt dull. He saw Port look at his watch while he held the phone, waiting.

"What time?" said Dicky.

"Time's up. Now."

Dicky saw Port purse his mouth, as if he were whistling. He was still holding the phone to his ear. Dicky felt the skin draw up on his scalp. He wanted to say something but he was afraid.

He saw that Port was frowning.

"Line's busy," said Port.

## *Chapter 20*

THE THREE MEN in the room never knew what had happened out in the hall; that Port had had to grab Dicky by the throat to keep him from screaming, that he had pressed him against the wall until Dicky had calmed down enough to listen to Port and to wait. Port had called again and this time there had been an answer. Port hadn't said much, just, "Where were you?" and "I know it was busy. All right. Never mind." Then he spoke the words that Dicky wanted to hear: "The deal's off. Don't call the police."

What the three men in the room saw was Port who looked at Dalton and smiled. "All right, Abe," he said. "Burn it." Dicky said nothing. What they didn't see was how Dicky felt, that he was alive again, hating Port and Dalton as he had never hated anyone before.

Dalton burned the notes on the stove and Dicky packed his bag. Mac didn't have one. He stood waiting for Dicky to finish. Loony sat at the table as before.

"I think I'll stay," he said. "I got an idea this job I got here—"

He let it go when Mac gave him a look. Mac's eyes were slitted from the swelling and his face was ugly. Then Dicky snapped the bag shut and straightened up.

"One more thing," he said to Port. "What about that loot?"

"I'll pick it up before you get there."

"And give it back?"

"How else do you think the cops are going to stop looking for it?" said Port.

Dicky shrugged, then jerked his head at Loony and Mac. Loony said again, "I think I'm staying," and watched Dicky anxiously, but there was no argument. Dicky didn't even look at Loony. He said, "Come on, Mac," and then went through the door. Mac went with him.

The room looked as if nothing had happened there. There was a man at the table who had just come from work, and a pot with a spoon on the stove, something left over from somebody's meal.

Port took Dalton's arm and led him out of the door. He nodded at Loony and Loony nodded back. Loony sat a while longer, until he heard the car pull away down the street. Then he ate what the old man had been cooking.

"I'll drive through the night," said Port. He watched the curve in the highway and waited until he hit the straight stretch again. "That way you can go back to the hospital in the morning."

"No," said Dalton. "Not there." He rested his head on the back of the seat and breathed slowly and carefully. "I'll go home now," he said. "Thank you, Port."

It was the only time Dalton had thanked Port, and it was enough.

Port said, "You think you're well enough?"

"It feels fair," said Dalton. "I can make it home." He paused. Then he said, "I had a letter from my nephew there, when I was still in jail. He says that they have a hospital now, new since I was there last."

"How long will you have to stay in it?"

"Maybe not at all. Maybe it'll heal at home."

"But you'll need a doctor, won't you?"

"I'll have a doctor. But I think it'll heal fine, when I get home."

"Yes," said Port and then they drove without talking.

Dalton was sitting up with one arm on the back of the seat, and he saw the lights first.

"A car's coming," he said.

Port looked in the mirror and nodded. "Yeah, I see it."

Dalton kept watching it. "It's coming very fast," he said. "Notice how fast."

Port looked in the mirror again.

"There are lots of cars faster than this one."

"And the lights," said Dalton. "He's got five lights in front."

Port said, "You mean Dicky Corday?"

"If he gets back to town first, I don't know—"

"You're worried he'll go for the loot I put in his room? Don't."

"Why? You don't have to bring it back? You paid for it?"

"No. I've got to return it, or pay for it."

The car had drawn close now.

"Can you tell?" asked Dalton.

The car behind swung into the passing lane and pulled away at a fast clip. The rear end seemed to be scooting along the ground and the two antennae in back weaved and dipped.

"That *was* Corday," said Port.

They watched the car move away fast. It had a bank of red and blue lights in the back. They got dimmer and then disappeared altogether.

"I don't want you to have any more trouble," said Dalton. "I wish you could get to town before he does."

"Look, Abe, he'd be a fool to go near that stuff. The way it's set up, the last place Dicky would want to go is his hotel room."

"And if he does?"

"They'll find him. He'll have walked into the frame of his own free will." Port looked at his watch. They had more than four hours to go. "I know he's crazy. But not that crazy."

It did not seem to concern Port and Dalton tried not to worry about it. After a while he slept. . . .

They reached town at eight in the morning, and when the car stopped at Dalton's place Port explained to him about Letty, how she had helped and that she was using his room. Dalton said that that was all right, and he wished he could do someting for the girl, now that it was over. She could keep the room, if she wanted to, and he would pay her a month's rent, because as for himself he was leaving now. He knew the train schedule by heart, and he could catch his train at noon. Dalton showed Port his ticket and when he put it back into his pocket and got out of the car, Port saw that the old man was smiling. He had not smiled since leaving the hospital.

The room was clean and Letty had made the bed. There was nothing lying around. Letty was gone.

Dalton sat down on the bed and unbuttoned his coat.

"I thought you said the girl was here."

"Yes. I thought so."

Dalton took his ticket out of his pocket and put it on the table next to his bed. Then he took off his coat and his shoes.

"She left nothing here?"

Port shook his head. He was walking around the room. He stopped at the window and looked out.

"I would like to offer her—as I said— If she wants this room—"

"Fine," said Port, and came back to the bed. "Maybe I'll see her. If I do I'll give her your message." He pulled a blanket back on the bed and motioned to Dalton. "You lie down now. Get some sleep, and I'll wake you when I come back."

Dalton lay back. He stretched out and looked up at the ceiling. He was smiling again.

"I won't see it much longer, the crack up there. You know, when I took this place after coming out, this room and the things here—the crack, the window with the rattle in it—all that looked so good to me. After ten years." He folded his hands on his stomach and looked at Port. "And now I'm leaving." He laughed shortly. "I'm just going to lie here now, Dan, and feel sentimental. You know? I can lie here and afford to feel sentimental." He laughed again and watched Port go to the door.

"I'm picking up the stuff from Corday's place. I'll drive you to the station when I come back."

Dalton had closed his eyes. He just nodded. When Port was halfway through the door he called after him, "And if you see that girl, tell her—"

Port left. When he got into his car he was whistling. He looked at his watch, started the car, and made a sharp U-turn.

The pickup wouldn't take long, less than an hour. Port drove, whistling tunelessly.

He wondered where Letty was. He wished he knew her better and did not have to wonder about her. On the way to Dicky's hotel he passed the Off-Time, where Dicky had cornered him in the alley. The big building was closed now.

He wondered where Letty was.

Past the next corner he remembered the other place, Nick's Palace or something, and the woman with the old face who liked nothing better than dancing, and who knew everybody. Nick's Palace was right, because Port could see it now. The neon sign was on. From here to the hotel it took about five minutes' driving. Perhaps the woman who knew everybody was in the bar. Perhaps she knew where Letty was.

Port stopped the car in front of the bar. If he did not find the woman here it would not make any difference, one way or the other. The hotel was down the next street. He would go there next.

At the hotel, Dicky Corday told Mac to stand by the door to the hall and he himself had gone into the bathroom. He knelt on the floor next to the sink, but he could not get the plumbing door open. Mac could hear him rattling the wood and cursing. Mac stood by the door with nothing to do, waiting and listening to Dicky in the bathroom. Mac's face hurt worse than ever now, and sounds set his teeth on edge. He could hear every footstep down on the street and a car coming by, or stopping, made him jump.

"Dicky. Hey. You getting anywhere?"

There was no answer, just the scraping behind the closed door and Dicky's cursing, low and intense. Mac looked out along the corridor and then he closed the door. There had been nothing out there and the waiting was getting him. He went to the bathroom and looked in. It made Dicky jerk around suddenly so that he hit his head on the edge of the sink.

"Don't get so jumpy," said Mac. He was whispering. He kept saying this while Dicky swore at him and until Dicky turned back to the small door.

"Aren't you done yet?" said Mac, leaning closer.

"Get back to the door." Dicky didn't look up. He was whispering like Mac and breathing hard from the effort of trying to pry at the door.

"There's a screw; don't you see the screw?"

"Shut up, willya?"

"Stop prying the edge there. Try—"

Dicky looked up. He thought he had never seen a face as ugly as Mac's. The two men glared at each other without saying a word. Then Corday turned away abruptly. There was no time.

He had a knife in his hand, and he went on prying at the edge of the door.

"If we had a screwdriver—" said Mac.

"Get my coat. I mean get the gun in my coat. Over there on the chair."

Mac brought the gun, a short Smith and Wesson with a gunsight that looked like a big, stiff fin. Dicky took the gun and worked the sight into the screw.

"Does it give?"

Corday was grunting.

"Try the knife on that—"

"Shut up. It's coming." Slowly, with an effort that made both of them hold their breath, the screw gave in small fractions.

"Now try the knife. Maybe with the screw loose now—"

Dicky picked up the knife and tried that. "Get back to the door," he said.

Mac stayed. He was watching the screw come loose slowly. The crack in the small door showed black now, like a wedge. Dicky dropped the knife and squeezed his fingers into the crack. Then he strained.

"There's another one, another screw, here on the bottom."

"I'm breaking it out. Here, get your hands in there—"

They both pulled now. The effort agonized their faces.

"Watch it. Now—"

"Not that way. Here. Try here!" The wood gave with a sudden snap.

They both fell backward and Corday, in his scramble to get back to the hole, jabbed Mac's face with his elbow. He had not even known he had done it until he heard the groan. And then Mac hit him.

They fought in the small space between the bathtub and the sink. They fought silently, a grotesque straining without motion.

A door slammed, down the hall, and both men jerked apart.

They had not even seen the loot yet. They did not even know if it was there. Corday reached into the hole and felt the pipes. Mac had stood up. He wanted to run to the door but first he wanted to see the loot.

"Well? Come on!"

"Wait," said Dicky. "Wait." The word seemed to help him search. There were pipes, one big and one small, going off to one side. And a valve, it felt like a valve with a string holding a bag—a string holding a bag! Then . . .

Dicky yanked and the thing came out, a small bag which looked lumpy inside.

They both rushed into the room and over to the table. Corday said, "Check the door; lock the door," and Mac said, "Open it up, on the table. Open it—"

Corday tore the string to get at the inside.

First there was a wad of odd bills.

"What he say, five thousand? Man, look at that!"

And then a tangled pile of jewelry with the hard, expensive glitter of real gems.

"Twenty-five grand worth? Twenty-five grand worth is what?"

"What?"

"Under the counter!"

"Hell, I can take it to Wint and—"

"You nuts or something? That guy's a crook, nothing but a crook. We're taking the stuff to—"

"Polly. She's got a good outlet where—"

"And cut her in? Listen—"

"You trying to tell me—"

They both stopped at once, turned to the door at once, and knew at once what was coming. Mac got to the door. Dicky ran to the bathroom to get his gun. Mac wanted first crack at Port and was pulling a spring knife from his belt when the door made a sound. It looked as if Mac was drawing a gun. Dicky came back into the room, the gun held behind him so that Port wouldn't see it. His grin was big.

One cop was in mufti, the other one in uniform. Each held a gun.

It wasn't real to Dicky until the shot. The bullet hit Mac. Mac, with his hand on the knife looking as if he were drawing a gun, caught the slug full in the shoulder. He spun back into Dicky and with a last effort swung up the arm with the knife so that the cop shied and shot a second time.

The knife sliced Dicky under the ear as Mac fell. Not dead yet, Mac clawed at the man behind him.

They fell together, one dead the other one stiff with the fear in his bones.

"Got them both," said the cop in uniform.

"Jesus. I didn't think—"

"Look, here's the jewels and everything on the table."

"Jesus!" said the other one, and the voice was close to Dicky now. "I got both of them—"

"The chest. And the other one in the neck. He still bleeding?"

"Jesus!" said the near voice again and then the feet went toward the bathroom, where water started to run.

Dicky lay still. He felt his gun under him, pressing into his belly. If nobody moved them— Don't think. Just lie still and live, lie still and let the strength bunch up in a ball to get ready.

There was the sound of feet again for a moment. There was talk. "Get the rest—tell Jack to call in for an ambulance—" Then he heard just one pair of shoes making a slow creak near the window. Corday saw the heels. The toes were pointed toward the wall under the window.

They swiveled around very fast then, but Dicky shot the cop dead. Before the body fell Dicky was running.

## *Chapter 21*

THE WHORE recognized Port before he was sure it was she. He went to her booth when he saw her wave, and then he saw why he hadn't been sure. Her hair was tied back and she wasn't wearing any make-up.

"The dancing fool," she said and grinned at him. "You come to see me?"

"Yes," said Port.

It surprised her. She looked down at her beer and her hand went up to her hair.

"You know," she said, "at eight or nine in the morning I usually just don't do nothing at all. I usually only—"

"I just want to talk," said Port. "Buy you a beer?"

"Oh," she said. "No, thank you. You don't have to buy me a beer."

Port said he knew that and he was sorry if it had sounded wrong, but he would like her to have a fresh beer if she wanted one, because he was going to have one too. Then they both waited for their fresh beers and the whore saw that Port was nervous.

"You don't have to wait," she said. "Ask me."

The beers came. Port paid for them and said, "I'm looking for a friend of mine who—"

"Same one?"

"Huh?"

"Dicky Corday."

"No. Letty."

"You was looking for Letty last time I seen you."

"That's right," said Port. "I was. I'm looking for her again."

"That's real steady of you," said the woman. "It's been days." She was grinning at him when she said it, but she was not especially friendly—or helpful, thought Port.

"Then you know who I mean," he said. "Have you seen her around?"

"Off and on. Why?"

Port said, "I've seen her in the meantime, since I talked to you last. But I've been out of town and when I came back we missed each other."

"Oh. Yeah. I see what you mean." She took a long pull at her beer. "That little girl's got a lot of admirers."

It was too much talk with no results. Port moved in his seat and coughed. When he looked up at the woman he sounded different.

"Look," he said. "There may be trouble. That's why I'm looking for her."

"In that case," said the woman, "maybe Letty better not show."

"All right," said Port. "You know where she is and you don't want her harmed." He picked up his beer and drained it.

"Who are you?" said the woman.

Port put his glass down and said, "Daniel Port." He looked at his watch and made a move to get out of the booth.

"Oh," said the woman. "You're the one!"

Port looked at the woman.

She said, "So you're the one been cutting in on poor Dicky." She watched him after that. She saw he wasn't patient enough now to explain himself and that he wanted to leave.

"No. You got that wrong." He got up. "You say Letty's all right?"

The woman smiled and nodded. She motioned for Port to sit down again. "I know I had it wrong," she said. "If you weren't Port I think you would have said something else."

Port sat down again, because now the woman was going to talk. He was still anxious to leave but it wouldn't take long.

"You know," said the woman, "I told you once how I've known the girl for a long time. Used to know her mother." She lit a cigarette and talked through the smoke. "So naturally, when the girl don't feel good or something like that, she comes to me."

"I understand," said Port. "I'm glad she has somebody."

"Yes," said the woman. "And she's told me about you."

"She was supposed to be somewhere when I came back. So when she wasn't there—"

"She's with me. She'll be all right. When that little girl has troubles—"

"What happened?"

The woman looked at her beer. She shrugged. "Ever since she was a baby, she's always been stubborn. It comes over her, and when she don't want to talk she won't talk." She leaned over the table and pushed the beer out of the way. "She's in bed now, sleeping. She come over in the middle of the night, practically, and I can see she's upset. I try talking to her, asking her, and she starts crying. She cried a long time."

"I'm sorry she's so upset. I—"

"No, no. That's all right. If she can't talk about it, it's good if she can cry about it."

"I tell you," said Port. "I made her do a few things, I don't think she was used to anything like it."

"I know. She isn't. She told me that part."

"That part?"

"She didn't tell more. There is more, though," said the woman. "All I know is, she's afraid of Dicky now. I don't mean like before, I mean real afraid. And even of you."

"Me?" Port frowned. A hundred pieces of doubt came together and made one large fear in Port.

"She won't say what but it's something she done."

"Christ!" said Port. He got out of the booth and wanted to run. "Look, you keep that girl where she is, hear? Don't let her out till I tell you. Where do you live?"

The woman told him.

"And don't tell anyone else, understand?"

"I'll take care," said the woman and then Port was gone.

He did not get into the car. He saw that he would only get stuck further up because there was a crowd in front of the hotel. He ran down the street and saw the ambulance. It took off before Port got there and the police cars took off too and a lot of cops spread out the length of the street. Port reached the nearest policeman and then he got stopped.

"Who are you?"

Port told him.

"Identification?"

Port showed him.

"All right. Now keep walking," said the cop.

"One get away?" Port asked. It did not sound casual.

"Not for long." The cop started walking.

"Which one?"

"The son of a bitch that didn't get shot."

Dicky, or Mac.

It was close to ten. Better get Dalton. Better make sure about Letty and then take care of Dalton. His train did not leave till twelve.

## *Chapter 22*

WHEN Abe Dalton woke up he knew immediately where he was, for how much longer he would be here, and that the next bed he'd sleep in would be one at home. He smiled at the ceiling, where the crack was, and when he heard the steps in the hall he smiled at the door. He said, "Come in," before anyone had knocked, because he felt relaxed after his sleep. "The door's open, Dan," he said and watched for the handle to turn.

It snapped over, the door opened and shut, and Dicky Corday was in the room.

Dalton stared. He could not sit up for the moment. Dicky Corday leaned against the door. His breathing was labored. When Dalton sat up he saw blood down the side of Dicky's neck, dirt on his face, and dirt on his hands. Then Dicky came over to the bed and took Dalton by the front of the shirt. He pulled the old man up until he was very close. Then he spat in Dalton's face.

Dalton sat down on the bed. He did not wipe the spittle off his face until much later.

"The old bastard with the word as good as gold," Dicky said. "The filthy old son of a bitch learning the double-cross this late in life." Dicky stared at Dalton, hoping for one wrong move.

There was nothing but blank confusion in Dalton's face.

Dicky sucked in his breath. "I walked into that frame! Cops, loot, and everything!"

"What?" Dalton was up.

"Didn't work, did it? Because I got away! And right now I'm here, so—"

"You mean—you mean Dan hadn't called the thing off?"

"There was cops waiting and cops chasing and Mac got shot in the head and you got the nerve to ask—"

"No! It's a mistake. Something went wrong—"

"You're damn right something went wrong. And you, Dalton, you're gonna make it right!"

"Dan wouldn't pull—"

"And maybe you didn't know about this?"

"No, Dicky. Nothing!"

"And I'm telling you they sprung it on me! And you—you're in on that double-cross."

"Are they after you?"

"What do you think they do when a cop killer gets away, huh?"

"No—"

"Yes! And you got to make it good, Dalton, fast."

"What—"

"I need dough. I got to get out of the city. You catch on, don't you?"

"You need my money? I have—"

"You know what day this is, Dalton? Thursday! Thursday night they put the money in the safe back in Newton. Follow me, Dalton?"

"Dicky, listen—" Dalton was up, his voice high. "You can't do it like this. You're running, you got no tools, the job needs— I've been telling you it needs much better planning. You got to—"

"That's what I got you for, Dalton. Come on. Move." Dicky's gun was out, nodding at Dalton.

The old man did not have the strength to argue. He leaned on the small table next to his bed and shook his head.

"Dicky, I'm too tired to be pushed any more. You can push and nothing would happen. I'm too tired."

He was not surprised when Dicky put the gun away. He was not surprised when Dicky changed his style and talked rapidly in the urgent tone he had used before, pleading with Port and trying to trade Letty.

"They're gonna have a ring around this town like a vise. I can still make it. I slipped the neighborhood where they're looking. Get me out, Dalton. I got a car I can use. You can drive. Me in the trunk and you driving—"

"I'm slow. I'm slow, Dicky. If you need a wheel man—"

"I don't need a wheel man, you stupid jerk, I need you! We're going to Newton and make it!"

"Dicky—"

"Now you hear this," said Dicky. His voice was suddenly low, and he was spacing his words. "You gave me your word; remember? And I went along. I traded you one frame for another. Your word wasn't good, Dalton, was it?" Dicky waited.

"No," said Dalton. "It wasn't good."

"You doublecrossed me, Dalton. I'm running now, and it's your fault. I'm running and I need your help because your word wasn't good."

When Port slammed into the room he saw that for the second time in a day he had been too late. There was one chair and Port sat down in it for a moment. He took a deep breath to slow himself down, and rubbed his hands over his face. Then he looked around the room again. The bed showed where a man had been lying on it, the hook on the door was empty, the railroad ticket lay on the table next to the bed. Dalton would only have forgotten it if there had been no point in remembering it.

Port got up. He went over to the table and picked up the ticket and stuffed it into his pocket. He did it with a violence that showed how the tension inside was growing stronger. When his hand was in his pocket he felt the gun. He took it out, flicked the cylinder open, and counted the shells even though he knew the gun had not been fired. Then he stuck it into his belt and buttoned his jacket.

Mac or Corday? It would help to know which, because one of the two would take Dalton back to the plant in Newton.

Port went out of the room and downstairs. His heels made hard clicks.

He could call the hospital and find out who had been admitted, shot up. It would take a while to find the right hospital. He could call the morgue, he could call the police, he could call the man he knew here in town, or he could ask almost anyone on the street in Dicky's neighborhood. For that matter, he could ask anyone who had been listening to the radio. The landlady's room was on the ground floor and the old lady was sweeping the hall. She had left her door open and the radio was droning on, something about soap so pure—

"You been listening to the news?" Port asked the woman.

"Couldn't help it," she said. "They even cut in on my program."

"About the shooting on the South Side?"

"Yes. One got away."

"Which one?"

"I don't know, but I know which one got killed."

"Who?"

"Maximilian Kloos. And one of the detectives got killed, by the one who got away. The detective's name was—"

"Thank you," said Port, and was gone.

Maximilian Kloos. Not Dicky Corday. Port got into his car, slammed the door, and punched the starter. Dicky Corday was out of town on his way to Newton with the old man—because this was Thursday, when they put the money into the safe.

The car tore away from the curb. Port didn't slow down until he got near the center of town. Traffic was heavy here and he had to crawl. The same would have happened to Dicky. Maybe he was still in town, lying low, waiting. That wouldn't make sense. This was Thursday, and he had Dalton along at the point of a gun.

The car was in low, whining, crawling.

Port wasn't the only one looking for Corday. The police were looking, an army of them, because of Port's own maneuver and because Corday had killed a cop.

And Abe Dalton was in the middle of it—unless Port got there first.

The light turned green but by the time Port reached it it had turned red again. He kept his foot on the throttle, gunning the motor in short, fast jabs. The light changed finally, and Port crossed the intersection, then crawled again, joining the traffic. He turned the radio on and he turned the dial till he found the station for police calls.

". . . two, eight, eight. No activity, over," and without pause, "Central to two, eight, eight. The accident is on corner Field and Bennington. Correcting previous instructions, corner Field and Bennington. Bicycle and truck. Over, out."

It crackled and went dead. Truck hit bicycle. Port fiddled with the knobs and heard music. He found his station again and heard, ". . . tow truck. We blew a tire. Over."

They blew a tire. Some cruiser was parked somewhere waiting for a tire. Nothing about Corday. Perhaps they had him. Perhaps— He fiddled with the dial some more and that was when he found the other station.

They were using two wave lengths.

". . . gray-blue Buick, fifty-six. License number LF twelve. Reported stolen in Sector B. All cars not on regular assignment abandon Sector B, proceed to M. Buick reported in Sector M. Fugitive believed to be driving stolen Buick, gray-blue, fifty-six, license number LF twelve. Observe extreme caution. Fugitive is armed. All cars . . ."

They had him tagged!

Loud horns made Port look up. He was still crawling, but the street ahead was clear and he was holding up a line of cars behind him. Port drove faster.

". . . cover Brook Road, Harwood, Eighth—"

Where was that?

". . . confirmed in Sector M. Fugitive last seen in Sector M—" A crackle, then the voice. "Correction. Last report from Sector Q. All odd numbers from Sectors O, P, R, proceed to Q. The fugitive is armed. Observe—"

Port's hand slipped on the wheel from sweat. They had him tagged, but where? The more he listened, the more they told him, and none of it meant a thing. Port was heading out now, going faster, going fast and straight to Newton while Corday and the old man were some place in a police grid sector in the city, which they might never leave.

He had to get to Dalton first!

Port hit the brakes and pulled in to the curb. He stopped beside the policeman.

"Officer!"

The cop was big and bored. He turned to look at Port and chewed his gum.

"Officer, I'm from the Courier; my name is Port." Port held out a card which he stuck back into his pocket when the cop moved closer.

The press? The cop stopped chewing gum and came up to the car. The press, on this beat? The cop smiled down at Port.

"Need some help?"

"I do. You heard about the cop killer loose in Sector Q?"

"Q? I didn't know he was in Q. The one shot his way outa that hotel on the South Side?"

"Right. He's in Q, and I'm supposed to cover that. Where's Q, officer? I've got to . . ."

The cop spat out his gum and looked animated.

"You sure? Christ, you're in it! Where'd you hear it, on the radio? Come on, come on, turn that thing up!" The cop leaned through the window.

". . . North Trumbull, South Trumbull, Ward Street, covered as requested. Over." And without pause, "Central to all cars. Follow plan W . . ."

There was more that Port did not understand. The cop was leaning in at the window and unwrapping some more gum listening to the radio and playing cops and robbers.

Port felt like screaming. The more he listened the more

he knew, and the more they could tell him, the more *they* knew!

But Port had to get to Dalton first! If he could find out which way they were going, what chance Corday had of getting away—

". . . Sectors S and T," said the voice.

"What now? You know what that means?" Port asked the cop.

"Hold it, just hold it—"

". . . plan W in Sectors S and T. Call Precinct Thirty for local instructions. Out."

"Boy!" said the cop.

"Well? Christ, don't let me sit here and—"

"You gonna mention in your column who give you the information?" said the cop. He offered Port a stick of gum.

"Hell, yes, I'd be pleased to, but let's have it."

"S and T, that's further out. See this?" The cop drew a circle on the windshield. "That's the city. You're here, the Highland district, what we call Sector Q, or part of it, anyway. Pretty far out, you see that?"

"Christ, yes. Come on, come on."

"That's out of the city!"

"Suburbs. Now you wanna know what they mean by plan W?"

Port groaned and nodded.

"That means all procedures relative to roadblock techniques. What we mean by that—"

"You mean roadblocks out there, out of the city?"

"Like I told you. He's heading out, the way Central describes it. Now, what we mean by roadblock—"

"So where's he going, heading that way?"

Port was very anxious now. He knew one town that lay out in that direction.

"Open country. He can take Highway Ten or alternate Twenty. One goes to Pittering and the other joins Six further south."

If Corday made it he would take Ten. He would take a cutoff to Newton before reaching the cross-country highway.

"That means they're bound to stop at the edge of one of those two sectors."

"Maybe."

"There're only two highways, you say—"

"But the country starts there. Remember what it said, to call the precinct for local dope? That's so the local men can direct the search out there, seeing there's open country and small roads and that kind of thing. You can't have a roadblock on a field, you know, and if that cop killer should—"

"I get it," said Port and shifted his gears.

"Now, I was telling you about this procedure we—"

"Look, thanks a lot, officer, thanks—" Port started moving.

The last thing Port heard was the cop yelling his name so that Port could put it in the paper.

If all this information were correct he would hit a roadblock in less than half an hour.

The cop's story was true. The roadblock itself was an impressive affair of six cars and/scores of troopers and city police equipped with riot guns, lights, and a radio truck. It meant that they didn't have Dalton and Corday yet. It might mean the pair had turned back; it might mean they were trying some other way.

The police had been looking for them on the South Side when Port had been halfway into the middle of town. Then they had switched to a sector far away in alphabetical order. Corday had a good start. He might make it.

When Port went through the roadblock they warned him about taking the trip.

Corday might make it. Even the police thought he might. Port drove off, and, hours later, when it was dark, he turned off on the road going to Newton. There were no more patrol cars racing by, no more motorcycles. The police wave length had long since died out and the calls from the highway stations had made no sense to Port.

The dark country rolled and the air smelled of rain. Port drove steadily. The wind shot past the windows and killed every other sound, except for Port's whistling, an irritating, unfinished sound. He kept it up far into the night. He didn't stop until he saw the Newton Plant, big and black on the landscape. Then he stopped whistling. He parked before the street ended and walked down the highway where the country began.

The plant looked bigger in the dark than it did in the daytime. Three lights in the court gave a dank, deserted look to the place. For some reason Port could smell hay.

The grilled gate was shut. Port took out his revolver and looked at the gate.

## Chapter 23

THEY STOOD in the dark and talked in whispers. The small light was on the dial.

"My hands aren't good enough any more," said Dalton. "Even if there were no timer."

There was silence, except for Dicky's breathing and Loony's feet shifting. Dalton was making no sound.

"Well? Don't gimme no list of what you can't do. There's something like thirty-five grand on the other side of this door and you stand there—".

"Be quiet," said Dalton.

Dicky was quiet. Dalton was working, and his voice was authoritative, without emotion.

"We have no tools," Dalton said.

"You think I was gonna stop and—"

"That means we have to find what we need here in the shop. Loony?"

"Yes," said Loony.

"A tank of acetylene, two of oxygen. If they're the big ones, just one each. Bring two torches and a handful of extra heads, new ones."

"I know where they are."

"A ball peen and wedge. Find some punches. Here. They have to fit here." Dalton pointed. "And a chisel, twelve-inch, and a sledge."

"Whyn't you go down with him and get it?" said Dicky.

Dalton ignored Dicky.

"Biggest electric drill you can find, and a handful of bits—quarter-inch, nothing bigger. And high carbon. Unless you got something harder?"

"We got. I know where."

"And lubricant, mixed well. That's all."

Loony left.

"You go with him," said Dicky. "That dumb ox—"

"Please. Let me sit."

Dicky had the light off and he couldn't see Dalton's face, only his outline as he sat down on a chair near a desk that stood by the window. Dicky saw how careful the movement was. He heard Dalton breathe carefully.

"You all right?" said Dicky.

Dalton ignored it. "I want you to take that light," he said, "and find the power line that goes into the alarm. It'll be sheathed. You can—"

"I know what I'm looking for."

"Find where it comes out of the main line. Or find out if it's independent."

Dicky didn't argue. He left. The old man stayed there and tried not to move. He was facing a window. It was very large, and he could look very far out over the countryside. He saw changing shades where fields must be, and thick black which had to be woods.

He turned back to the room. It was darker there, and it would help to get used to the darkness.

Dicky was the first one back.

"It came out of a main," he said. "I jumped it."

Dalton said, "The next time I tell you to check, just check. You don't—"

At first the voice had been clipped but then it faltered after a sudden hesitation. Dicky didn't know why, but Dalton did. He had said, "The next time."

"Go help Loony with the tanks," Dalton said wearily.

Dicky left and Dalton sat in his chair. His head was down as if he were looking at his hands. He could see nothing and he had stopped thinking. There was nothing to think about. He was doing this job and there was nothing to think about.

They made quite a racket returning with the tanks. They brought those and the other things Dalton had wanted. They dropped everything at the door of the safe and Dalton got up and went over to them.

"Plug in the drill," he said.

Then he picked out a bit and set it into the drill. "Ready there?"

"I got it plugged in," said Loony.

"All right. Dicky, get set with the coolant, and you, Loony, stand outside."

Dicky held the can of lubricant ready and Dalton flicked the drill trigger a few times. It made a high, noisy whirr. Loony went out through the door. He stood on the dark stairs where he could see the entrance to the office building and the metal stairs that went down to the shop. He stood there and lit a cigarette.

Then Loony's cigarette jumped out of his mouth.

Port caught him from behind. Port lowered him gently, felt the back of his head, and then straightened up with a faint sound of exhaling.

The swinging door to the room with the safe had large glass panels on it. Behind it was the dark room, the shadow of desks, and the bright, busy spot of light. Dalton was raising the drill, using both hands. Dicky held the light in one hand and the oil can in the other. He would drop the light first.

There were two sharp whirrs from the drill and when the sound died the drill went into position.

"Now," said Dalton.

"Drop it!"

For a long, still instant there was nothing, just the sigh of the swinging door behind Port.

Dicky dropped the light and scuttled away from the safe. He was not very fast. The shot rang out before the sound of his movement was over.

Silence.

"You shoot often enough, Corday, and they'll hear you in town."

Dicky used all the profanity he could think of, cursing into the dark at Port. But he did not know where Port was.

When it was over the scene was as before. Dalton had not moved. The light was still at his feet. It shone at the safe and it highlighted Dalton's face with a weird effect of long shadows running up his features.

"Dan!"

It was hard to tell what the intonation in the voice meant. It was not relief and it was not a question.

"You move, Dalton," said Dicky, "you move or kick that light and you're dead. Port! You hear that?"

Port didn't answer. There was no point.

"Now get up, Port. You hear me?"

Port told Dicky what he could do.

"Quiet, both of you!"

They both listened to Dalton. They both strained into the dark as if Dalton might solve everything.

"Go away, Dan."

"Tell him to throw out his rod," said Dicky.

"Quiet," said Dalton.

It was the light, Port thought, the way it hit Dalton's face from below. His face was set, without movement.

"Dan," said Dalton. "I want you to go away."

"You're rattled," said Port. "Just stand still. I'm—"

"No, Dan. It's no use."

"Abe, I know he's got a gun on you now, but—"

"He can put the gun down if he wants. I'm staying. I'm going through with the job."

## *Chapter 24*

PORT felt as if he had been hit. He caught his breath and held so still behind his desk that the gun in his hand started to tremble.

"Dalton," he said. "You're out of your mind."

Dalton lowered the drill and held it along his side. He turned slightly, so that Port could see him full-face.

"You sprung that frame on Corday. I won't take that, Dan. I gave my word."

"Abe, for God's sake don't talk like an idiot. You had nothing to do with that! A slip-up. A bad slip-up but you had nothing to do with it!"

"I gave my word," said Dalton and turned back to the safe. "I haven't much else." He lifted the drill.

"Abe! Listen!" Port yelled, but the drill was going with a hard whine and Dalton aimed at a spot near the dial. The sound of the drill would change when he set it into the metal. He was cautious about it, and precise. It drew Port's eyes, made him watch—and the same would happen to Corday. Dalton was aiming the drill and Corday must be watching— Port jumped. The wall wasn't far behind him. Port hit the switch near the door, flicked it, and when the ceiling lights came on Port was down on the floor again.

Dicky's shot broke the glass in the swinging door. Then he shot twice more, at the light in the ceiling. One fluorescent tube shattered, but there were nine more of them.

"Kill that light, damn you! The whole town can see it!"

"Right," said Port.

Dalton had dropped the drill. He looked sick in the white light. He was leaning against the safe, shaking his head. His eyes seemed to be closed.

Port forgot about Dalton then. His turn would come later. Corday was cursing across the room and his feet made sliding noises. Port lay down on the floor, flat, his head sideways. Then he aimed and shot Corday in one foot.

It couldn't have been very bad. Corday yelled, started scrambling, and ran crouched along the far wall. He reached a partition with a door that said *Private* and when Port shot again the door slammed shut with a hole in it.

Somebody would see the light.

The office and the partitions were like a maze, and both men had to go by sound, Port after Corday and Corday running to find a way out.

He made it. Port heard him in the hall, where Loony was lying, and then he heard the fast click of heels on metal steps.

Port ran back into the office. Dalton was sitting now. He had slid down along the door of the safe and he was sitting on the floor where the tools were lying.

"Abe. Up! Take my hand—"

Dalton didn't raise his hand. He sat slumped, shaking his head.

"Abe, damn it, you're coming with me!"

Port had to drag him. He had Dalton halfway up on his shoulder when the siren cut loose back in town.

Not the shop stairs—too narrow— Port made it down, sliding and stumbling, and crashed into the door that led outside.

A laugh. Somebody laughed in the yard. Then Corday fired from the truck ramp. Unless he had reloaded he had only one shot left.

The siren got bigger and much more urgent. Two sirens now!

Port thought he saw Corday in the yard, but they had to get out now.

"Left," said Dalton. "There is a way left—better—"

Port dragged Dalton through the door and went left. He would have to cross where a yard light was. Dalton was wrong. Then Port saw Corday run through a light on the right and disappear behind the edge of a building. Port ran, dragging. Past the light there were no buildings, a fence— Too much in the open.

"Keep going," Port heard. "There is a fence close."

Port couldn't see it.

Then he did, as if it jumped at him, jumped with the reflection on wire loops along the whole width of vision. Port let Dalton drop and threw himself down next to him.

Behind them, off to one side, the yard near the gate suddenly exploded into brilliance. Two lights on the towers that held the gate and lights from the road on the other side went on. The space looked huge and bare and Dicky Corday was in it. He stopped dead and then waved his arms as if fighting the beams. He had one shot left. He fired. A light went out on one tower. Corday cursed and screamed in the empty yard and then tossed his gun away.

He didn't hit anyone. The men running at him had Corday in a circle. It was over.

Port and Dalton got over the fence where trucks were parked. The trucks made the climb possible. Port and Dalton made it across a wild field, through muddy water and around bushes. Then came a road, then the highway, and while Dalton lay in a ditch Port walked into town and got his car. He found Dalton where he had left him and they drove off.

Port didn't notice until they were far out of town and the car was roaring steadily along the black highway that Dalton was sick. His face was an inhuman gray and his skin was clammy with sweat. He sat doubled over, groaning.

"I'll stop, Abe, if you say the word. Can you hold out three hours until we get to the hospital?"

The old man did not answer.

There were just two small towns on the way, nothing

big enough for a hospital. But maybe there was a doctor.

"Abe. Another fifteen minutes and I'll be able to look for a doctor."

The old man just sat.

"Shall I stop? You want to rest?"

The old man would not talk. For the moment the pain seemed to have gone because he sat up and his face wasn't as strained as before. He looked straight ahead and would not answer.

"Abe, what is it? You talked before. You told me how to get away. What now?"

"I did not want to get caught," said Dalton.

It was a relief to hear him say something. Port took out a cigarette and lit it.

"You feel better?"

"Yes."

"Abe, if something's eating you—"

"I told you before, in the plant. What else is there to say?"

Port took a deep drag.

"It went wrong, Abe. I told you. I called the frame off, right there with Corday next to me. In that hallway, you remember?"

"I thought you had."

Port was very tired. He had not slept in two days and too much had gone wrong.

"I could tell you how it went wrong, how it wasn't my fault and why your word was good."

Dalton leaned over. He looked as if he were dizzy. He kept his head down and said, "I've never gone back on my word, Dan. And now, this late—"

"Look, Abe. You—"

Port stopped talking because Dalton was in no shape to listen. Dalton had winced and the movement forced a sound out of his throat. Then he leaned back, looking exhausted. When Port slowed, not knowing what to do, Dalton moved his head. He said, "Drive. No difference."

Port drove. He wanted to get to the hospital.

"Abe, I don't know about your condition. Is it dangerous to go on? Should I stop? Tell me."

"It makes no difference," said Dalton.

"Lean back more, over this way. Or do you want to lie on the back seat?"

There was a long moment before Dalton spoke. "Dan," he said, "I've been wrong all my life, but I don't think—" The rest died into a mumble.

Port knew there was only one thing to do—drive as fast as he possibly could. The car raced down the highway, chasing the beam that sliced the darkness ahead and it seemed as if the black road in front of the car had no end. The sound of the motor was like the roar of a fever and the speed was like a fever too.

"Almost," said Port, "almost there." He did not dare say how many hours it would take. He did not even look at his watch.

"All my life—" Dalton mumbled again.

"Abe, I know what's bothering you. But you didn't lie about the frame. Because I didn't. Abe, listen. If I had arranged it so Dicky got caught, would I have left you in your room, sleeping? Do you think I would have left you alone?"

Port tore around a curve, holding himself by the wheel.

"I'm all right," Dalton said. He sounded much better. "I believe you," he said, "because you didn't blame it on Letty."

Port looked sideways once but said nothing.

"I know she did it," said Dalton, "but you didn't blame it on her." He rested for a while and then said, "It will be hard on her. Perhaps—" His voice suddenly wandered and he said a few words that made no sense.

Port was afraid to talk to him.

Once Dalton said, "Hemorrhage—"

Port drove like fury.

Then Dalton tried once more. "It's all right now. I've been wrong, but I don't think I've—"

Then he fainted. He did not wake up, and Port chased the beam and the car seemed to swallow the road.

He slowed down later. He drove automatically at a sensible speed. When Port got to town with Dalton the old man was already cold.

Dan Port left the city very soon afterwards. He saw that Abe Dalton was buried, and he saw Letty once more. It was best that the girl should leave town. Abe Dalton had left a railroad ticket and Port had found the old man's five hundred dollars. He exchanged the ticket for Letty, to a town where she had some friends. And he gave her the money.

It reminded Port of the thing Dalton had done with Eve Simmon. He was sorry that Eve Simmon could not have helped. The old man, Port thought, had been wrong most of his life, but he had not been bad.

THE END

PETER RABE

# BLACK LIZARD BOOKS

**JIM THOMPSON**
*AFTER DARK, MY SWEET* $3.95
*THE ALCOHOLICS* $3.95
*THE CRIMINAL* $3.95
*CROPPER'S CABIN* $3.95
*THE GETAWAY* $3.95
*THE GRIFTERS* $3.95
*A HELL OF A WOMAN* $3.95
*NOTHING MORE THAN MURDER* $3.95
*POP. 1280* $3.95
*RECOIL* $3.95
*SAVAGE NIGHT* $3.95
*A SWELL LOOKING BABE* $3.95
*WILD TOWN* $3.95

**HARRY WHITTINGTON**
*THE DEVIL WEARS WINGS* $3.95
*FIRES THAT DESTROY* $4.95
*FORGIVE ME, KILLER* $3.95
*A MOMENT TO PREY* $4.95
*A TICKET TO HELL* $3.95
*WEB OF MURDER* $3.95

**CHARLES WILLEFORD**
*THE BURNT ORANGE HERESY* $3.95
*COCKFIGHTER* $3.95
*PICK-UP* $3.95

**ROBERT EDMOND ALTER**
*CARNY KILL* $3.95
*SWAMP SISTER* $3.95

**W.L. HEATH**
*ILL WIND* $3.95
*VIOLENT SATURDAY* $3.95

**PAUL CAIN**
*FAST ONE* $3.95
*SEVEN SLAYERS* $3.95

**FREDRIC BROWN**
*HIS NAME WAS DEATH* $3.95
*THE FAR CRY* $3.95

**DAVID GOODIS**
*BLACK FRIDAY* $3.95
*CASSIDY'S GIRL* $3.95
*NIGHTFALL* $3.95
*SHOOT THE PIANO PLAYER* $3.95
*STREET OF NO RETURN* $3.95

**HELEN NIELSEN**
*DETOUR* $4.95
*SING ME A MURDER* $4.95

**DAN J. MARLOWE**
*THE NAME OF THE GAME IS DEATH* $4.95
*NEVER LIVE TWICE* $4.95
*STRONGARM* $4.95
*VENGEANCE MAN* $4.95

**MURRAY SINCLAIR**
*ONLY IN L.A.* $4.95
*TOUGH LUCK L.A.* $4.95

**JAMES M. CAIN**
*SINFUL WOMAN* $4.95
*JEALOUS WOMAN* $4.95
*THE ROOT OF HIS EVIL* $4.95

**PETER RABE**
*KILL THE BOSS GOODBYE* $4.95
*DIG MY GRAVE DEEP* $4.95
*THE OUT IS DEATH* $4.95

**HARDCOVER ORIGINALS:**
*LETHAL INJECTION* by JIM NISBET $15.95
*GOODBYE L.A.* by MURRAY SINCLAIR $15.95

**AND OTHERS...**
FRANCIS CARCO • *PERVERSITY* $3.95
BARRY GIFFORD • *PORT TROPIQUE* $3.95
NJAMI SIMON • *COFFIN & CO.* $3.95
ERIC KIGHT (RICHARD HALLAS) • *YOU PLAY THE BLACK AND THE RED COMES UP* $3.95
GERTRUDE STEIN • *BLOOD ON THE DINING ROOM FLOOR* $6.95
KENT NELSON • *THE STRAIGHT MAN* $3.50
JIM NISBET • *THE DAMNED DON'T DIE* $3.95
STEVE FISHER • *I WAKE UP SCREAMING* $4.95
LIONEL WHITE • *THE KILLING* $4.95
JOHN LUTZ • *THE TRUTH OF THE MATTER* $4.95
ROGER SIMON • *DEAD MEET* $4.95
BILL PRONZINI • *MASQUES* $4.95
BILL PRONZINI & BARRY MALZBERG • *THE RUNNING OF BEASTS* $4.95
VICTORIA NICHOLS & SUSAN THOMPSON • *SILK STALKINGS* $16.95
*THE BLACK LIZARD ANTHOLOGY OF CRIME FICTION* Edited by EDWARD GORMAN $8.95
*THE SECOND BLACK LIZARD ANTHOLOGY OF CRIME FICTION* Edited by EDWARD GORMAN $15.95

Black Lizard Books are available at most bookstores or directly from the publisher. In addition to list price, please sent $1.00/postage for the first book and $.50 for each additional book to **Black Lizard Books, 833 Bancroft Way, Berkeley, CA 94710. California residents please include sales tax.**